THE VAMPIRE GAME

by

MARK LUKENS

Mark Lukens

Cover design by: Enchanted Whispers Art
http://www.enchanted-whispers.com

OTHER BOOKS BY MARK LUKENS

THE ANCIENT ENEMY SERIES
ANCIENT ENEMY
DARKWIND: ANCIENT ENEMY 2
HOPE'S END: ANCIENT ENEMY 3
EVIL SPIRITS: ANCIENT ENEMY 4

THE DARK DAYS POST-APOCALYPTIC SERIES
COLLAPSE: DARK DAYS BOOK 1
CHAOS: DARK DAYS BOOK 2
EXPOSURE: DARK DAYS BOOK 3
REFUGE: DARK DAYS BOOK 4
AFTERMATH: DARK DAYS BOOK 5
SURVIVORS: DARK DAYS BOOK 6
HELL TOWN: DARK DAYS BOOK 7
AVALON: DARK DAYS BOOK 8

NOVELS
SIGHTINGS
DEVIL'S ISLAND
WHAT LIES BELOW
DESCENDANTS OF MAGIC
THE SUMMONING
NIGHT TERRORS
THE EXORCIST'S APPRENTICE
POSSESSION: THE EXORCIST'S APPRENTICE 2
THE DARWIN EFFECT
FOLLOWED
SLEEP DISORDERS
GHOST TOWN: A NOVELLA
SLEEP DISORDERS

COLLECTIONS
A DARK COLLECTION: 12 SCARY STORIES
RAZORBLADE DREAMS: HORROR STORIES
FOUR DARK TALES

Mark Lukens

Special thanks to: Ann, Jet, Kelli, Valerie, and Mary Ann—your help is invaluable to me.

Mark Lukens

 ONE

THERON

Theron snapped awake when he heard his cell phone ringing. He sat up on the couch, pawing at the nearby table until he grabbed his phone. He squinted at the screen as the phone rang again—he didn't recognize the number. "Metcalf Investigations," Theron croaked into the phone after swiping the talk button.

"Is this Theron Metcalf?" a woman asked. She sounded young, and there was a tremor in her voice. Her words were hurried, everything coming out in a rush of breath. This woman was either nervous or scared.

"Speaking. Who is this?"

"My name's Cynthia Byers. My dad's friend Wally Chamberlain is a friend of yours. He recommended you."

Theron struggled to recall the name as he came fully awake. "Yeah, I know Wally."

"I need your help."

Theron stood up. A case—he hadn't had a case in a while and the bills had been mounting lately. "How can I help?"

"Can you meet me?"

"Tonight?" He glanced at his digital alarm clock. It was only nine thirty, but he had dozed off with the TV in the corner still on and the sound turned down low. "We could meet tomorrow at my office—"

"I'm at the Dairy Queen on Route 41 right now. It's about to close soon and I don't have a car."

Theron hesitated for a moment, about to speak, but then Cynthia spoke, cutting his words off. "Someone's been following me and I'm scared."

Theron paced the small back room he now called home with his phone up to his ear—it only took him six steps to get from one side of the room to the other. "Who's following you?"

"I don't have time to explain. Can you meet me here?"

"Did you call the police about this?"

"The police can't help me." She sighed in frustration. "Look, this is really complicated."

"Illegal?"

"No. I can explain everything if you'll come meet me. I looked up your website. I know you require three hundred dollars upfront. I have that with me. And I can pay whatever your daily pay is."

"It's a hundred dollars a day."

"Fine."

"Plus any extra expenses."

"That's fine."

"How old are you?"

"I'm eighteen."

"Your parents—"

"I can make my own decisions."

"Okay," Theron said, not too happy that she had just snapped at him.

"Sorry, it's just that my parents can't help, either," Cynthia continued in a more reasonable tone. "I don't want them involved with this."

Theron thought Cynthia's proposition over for a few seconds as he stood beside the small folding table that served as his dining room table. A small microwave oven was shoved against the wall on the other side of the table. He needed the money this job would bring, but something didn't feel right about this.

"Look, if you don't want to help, I understand," Cynthia said. "But I need someone's help before Damon kills somebody. Before he makes his first kill."

A chill skittered across Theron's skin. *First kill?* "Who's Damon? Is he the one following you?"

A pause from Cynthia. "No, it's not Damon this time. But there are others. I can explain everything when we meet. Please. The Dairy Queen's going to close at ten o'clock."

Theron still wasn't sure about this, but he could tell Cynthia was desperate and scared. "This person who's been following you, is he there right now?"

"I don't know. I think he might be."

"Stay right there," Theron told her. "I'll be there in twenty minutes."

"I'll be outside waiting for you."

"Okay. I'll be there as quick as I can."

"Thank you," Cynthia said and hung up.

Theron pressed the button to end the call. Cynthia said her dad was friends with Wally Chamberlain. Well, it was too late to start checking around on that connection, but for right now a recommendation from Wally was good enough for him. Besides, Theron's gut feeling told him this girl was in trouble, and he always trusted his gut feeling.

He shoved his socked feet into his shoes and slung his shoulder holster on, tightening it. He checked his .45 and shoved it down into the holster. He slipped his windbreaker on, concealing his weapon. He grabbed his car keys and headed for the door.

 TWO

THERON

When Theron got to the Dairy Queen, he saw Cynthia standing twenty feet away from the entrance; she was smoking a cigarette as she took cover from the rain under the overhang of the roof. She was dressed in layers of clothing with a black leather jacket over all of it. Theron parked his car and got out. He hurried through the drizzling rain to her. She looked as scared as she had sounded on the phone.

"Do you see him?" Cynthia asked before Theron could even get a word out.

"Who?"

She nodded towards the parking lot.

Theron turned and stared at the far end of the parking lot where no cars were parked. A man stood motionless in the rain, standing at the edge of the grass where it met the parking lot, staying far enough away from the streetlights to remain hidden in the shadows. The man was tall with broad shoulders, and it looked like he was wearing some kind of trench coat.

Theron looked back at Cynthia. "Is he the one following you?"

"He's one of them." Her eyes darted away from Theron—she was looking at her stalker again.

Theron looked back at the parking lot.

The man was gone.

No way the man could have gotten away that fast; there was nowhere for him to hide.

"We need to leave now," Cynthia said, on the verge of panic, drawing Theron's attention back to her. Cynthia's fingers trembled as she lifted the cigarette up to her lips. "He'll come back."

Theron looked back to where the man had been standing at the edge of the parking area a moment ago, trying to see where the man could have run to. Then he turned to Cynthia. "Come on. I know where we can go."

Cynthia got into Theron's car. Theron started his car and backed out of the parking space. He drove slowly around the Dairy Queen building, driving over to where the man had been, the headlights of his car washing across the edge of the parking lot and the grass of the hill that led down to the road below. There were no shrubs or trees in this area, nowhere the man could have hidden. It was bothering Theron that the man had disappeared so quickly.

"What's going on?" Theron asked Cynthia as he circled the building again. "Who was that guy? Why is he following you?"

"I'll tell you everything when we get somewhere safe. Can we just get out of here?"

Theron pulled out of the Dairy Queen parking lot and onto the street.

"That guy in the parking lot just now—was that Damon, the guy you were talking about on the phone earlier? The one you said might kill someone."

"No."

"But you said Damon's been following you, too?"

"Yes," Cynthia answered. "But that guy tonight, he was one of the other ones."

"Other ones?"

"They're trying to get me because I got out of the game."

"Out of the game? What game?"

"I promise I'll tell you everything when we get somewhere safe," she said. She stared straight ahead, staring out the windshield as Theron drove down the road through the rain, the windshield wipers thumping back and forth.

Cynthia turned around and looked out the rear window.

"We're not being followed," Theron said. "I've been watching."

She turned back around in her seat, facing forward again, finally calming down a little now that they were on the road.

But Cynthia's paranoia was getting to Theron a little; he found himself glancing at the rearview mirror just to be sure no one was tailing them. He got off the main drag through town and took some side roads to his office so he would be able to tell if they were being followed.

THREE

THERON

en minutes later Theron pulled up in front of his office, which was in the middle of a strip plaza. The long building of offices and stores was shrouded in darkness—all of the businesses closed for the night, the only lights coming from a line of streetlights along the road.

He parked his car in front of his office. METCALF INVESTIGATIONS, LLC was printed on the plate glass window in large letters, and again on the door along with contact information in smaller gold letters. He shut his car off and got out. He looked around on his way to the door, but he didn't see anyone lurking in the darkness.

Cynthia got out of the car and hurried to catch up to Theron. She'd hardly said a word on the drive there, and she was still glancing around, watching the road in front of the plaza.

"We weren't followed," he told her as he unlocked the glass door to his office and opened it. "I made sure of it."

After they were inside the office, Theron shut the door and locked it; the deadbolt made a satisfying snapping sound as it clicked into the metal doorframe. He flipped on the overhead lights, flooding the room with fluorescent light.

"Could we keep those off?" Cynthia asked him.

Strange request, but he turned them back off. He walked across his small office to the doorway that led to the back room where he lived now. He opened the door and turned on the light, then pulled the door almost all the way closed, providing enough light to see, but still keeping the office shrouded in darkness. "Is that okay?" he asked her.

Cynthia nodded as she sat down in one of the two matching chairs in front of his desk. His office consisted of a beat-up desk, his office chair, a filing cabinet, and the two chairs in front of the desk. There were a few paintings hung on the walls, a fake plant stuck in a corner, the plastic leaves coated with dust. He'd gotten almost everything in the office from the thrift store at the end of the plaza.

"You mind if I smoke?" she asked, already pulling out a pack of cigarettes from her purse, obviously ignoring the NO SMOKING signs by the door and on his desk.

Theron nodded at her, giving her the go ahead—she looked like she really needed a cigarette right now. "I used to smoke, but ever since I was diagnosed with a heart condition I had to give it up. Along with the booze."

Cynthia hesitated with an unlit cigarette in her hand. "Oh, I'm sorry." She was already poking the cigarette back into the pack.

"No, it's okay," he told her. "Go ahead and smoke. It won't bother me."

"You sure?"

He nodded.

She lit her cigarette.

Theron went into the back room. The couch he slept on was against one wall with a recliner right next to it. A small flat screen TV sat on a stand on the opposite wall. In another corner was a portable clothes rod with his extra suits and shirts hanging from plastic hangers. There was a small dresser with a few boxes of canned goods on top of it and his folding card table. All of the furniture jammed in the room made it seem even smaller and crowded, but also strangely cozy somehow.

He took off his windbreaker and hung it up on the back of the door. He grabbed two cans of Coke from the mini-fridge, a towel for Cynthia, and a small plastic bowl for her cigarette ashes and butts.

He had been staying in this back room since he'd lost his apartment a few months ago. He just needed a few more months to get back on his feet again, and this money from Cynthia would definitely help. At first he'd felt a little sleazy even thinking about taking money from a teenager, but now it wasn't about the money anymore—Cynthia was in some sort of trouble and she needed help. She was scared that people were following her, and Theron had seen somebody in the Dairy Queen parking lot tonight, there was no denying that. But what concerned Theron the most was this Damon person she had mentioned on the phone, the one who was supposedly going to kill someone soon.

He closed the door to the back room almost all the way again so they had enough light to see in the office, then he walked a few steps over to Cynthia and handed her the towel. "It's clean," he told her.

"Thanks," she said. She accepted the towel, but she didn't use it. She folded it over the arm of her chair.

Theron set the can of Coke and the plastic bowl down on the desk in front of her and then sat down in his office chair behind his desk.

Cynthia was a pretty girl, naturally beautiful, but she wore a mishmash of punk and gothic clothing that Theron felt was marring her looks. Her jeans had holes in the knees, and she wore a flannel shirt over a black T-shirt with the name of some rock band on the front, all of it under her black leather jacket that she hadn't taken off yet. Her fingernails were painted black, but the polish was beginning to wear off a little. She wore a lot of jewelry, most of it cheap silver stuff. She had a leather band on each wrist, one of them dotted with metal studs. Her makeup was dark and heavy, smeared a little now from her tears and the rain.

"Do you mind if I see some ID?" Theron asked. "Just standard protocol. I'll also have you fill out a couple of forms, but we can do that tomorrow."

Cynthia didn't seem to mind the request. She dug a pink wallet out of her small purse and opened it, plucking out her driver's license. She handed it to him across the desk.

Theron stared at the license for a moment. Cynthia looked a little younger in the ID photo, and she didn't have as much dark makeup on. And she looked happy. Smiling. "Thanks, Cynthia," he said and handed it back to her.

"Everybody calls me Cyn."

"Sin?" Theron asked.

"Yeah, Cyn. Short for Cynthia."

Theron just nodded. "Okay, Cyn." He cleared his throat a little. "I hate to ask, but do you have the—"

"Oh, the money," Cyn said. She seemed a little embarrassed that she had forgotten. She slipped her driver's license back into her pink wallet and pulled three one hundred dollar bills out and offered them to Theron.

"Thanks," Theron said. He pulled his own wallet out and slid the crisp bills into it. He pulled out a receipt book from a drawer and filled it out for her.

"How long have you been a private investigator?" she asked him as she inhaled another drag from her cigarette.

Theron handed the receipt to her, and then he popped his can of Coke open and took a sip. "Close to ten years now. I was a cop before this," he added, feeling the need to offer proof of his training and abilities. He'd gone to the police academy after four years in the Marines. He'd been a street cop for eight years until he made detective. He'd been good at his job, but in those last few years he had cut a few corners and there were a few "incidents" that caused him to "retire" early. At least he'd gotten a partial pension. Between that and the money he made as a P.I., he barely got by. Insurance for his car, his business, his health, all of it was eating him alive. Every time he turned around, his bills were going up. He'd been divorced twice, and taken to the cleaners twice.

"I'm good at what I do," he assured her.

Cyn didn't respond. She took another drag from her cigarette.

God, just the smell of the smoke was still tempting him. But he couldn't give in; he had wrecked his body enough with cigarettes and booze over the years. If he had any kind of a chance with the heart meds his doctor had prescribed to him, then he needed to stay away from the cancer sticks.

"Do you mind if I record this?" Theron asked, already opening a drawer to grab his digital recorder.

"I'd rather you didn't," she said.

Theron closed the drawer again—she seemed pretty firm about that. Instead, he grabbed a small notepad and a pen to jot down some notes. It was a little tough to see the paper in the murky light, but he would manage.

"Okay, Cyn. We're safe here. You said you would explain everything. Let's start with that guy in the Dairy Queen parking lot. Who was he?"

"You wouldn't believe me."

Theron didn't say anything for a moment, wondering if Cyn might be playing games now. But if she was, she was doing a hell of a job acting. No, Theron was sure Cyn was scared of something—terrified, actually.

"What about this Damon guy you told me about?" Theron asked. "The one you said was going to kill someone? You said something about a first kill. And you said that wasn't Damon in the parking lot tonight?"

"No. I already told you it was one of the others."

Theron sat back in his chair and sighed. This wasn't getting anywhere. "Okay. Why don't you tell me everything? Start at the beginning."

Cyn started talking.

#

CYN

When I first saw Damon Kurtz almost a year ago, I knew I had to have him. Me and my best friend Melony (but I always called her Mel) were at a house party she'd been invited to. There were some high school kids there like us, but most of the people there were a few years older than we were.

Damon, I would find out a short time later, was only two years older than me—nineteen years old when I met him at that party. But he seemed older than his years, wise and mystical, dark and brooding, dangerous.

This was a goth party. Mel had been into goth for over a year by then. She always dressed in black; she wore leather, black boots, corsets, ripped stockings, dark makeup and nail polish. She listened to punk and heavy metal music. I was dipping my toes into the goth world at that time, but not ready to take the plunge just yet. I'd seen how Mel got treated at school, the way the other girls looked at her. Of course Mel didn't care; it was almost like she thrived on the negative energy from others.

There were other goths at this party. Heavy metal music blasted from a stereo in the corner of the living room. There was a lot of drinking and smoking, a little bit of pot and ecstasy. There were only about thirty people there so I didn't feel too overwhelmed. I'd worn some black stretch pants and a black T-shirt. I used some of Mel's dark lipstick and eye makeup. But I still wasn't fitting in. My hair was blond. I had no piercings or tattoos. I felt like an imposter and swore I was getting that vibe from some of the other girls there.

But at least no one challenged me; they were cordial, possibly seeing a convert to their culture. Mel and I smoked cigarettes and mingled.

I'd never been much of a drinker, and Mel had driven there so she didn't want to drink. Her parents had handed down their Dodge minivan to her a year earlier when she'd turned sixteen. Mel's parents were pretty well-off and lived in a nice home on the north side of town. Mel's mom was a nurse and her dad used to do something in the banking industry, but now he was a pharmaceutical salesman—he was gone a lot of the time on business trips. Her parents were sweet and supportive of Mel. They felt it was important that Mel "find" herself and express herself. But Mel still found a way to fantasize that she struggled with her parents. She complained that her older brother was the "good child" of the family. He was away at college, getting a degree in finance, following in "Daddy's" footsteps as Mel liked to put it. Mel's parents always seemed overly-enthusiastic about her goth lifestyle, but the more they accepted it, the more it seemed to make her angry, like she was hoping to clash with them, always itching for an argument so she could prove to herself that she was some kind of rebel.

Mel was a few inches shorter than me and at least thirty pounds heavier. She was attractive in a plain sort of way, but there was nothing truly striking about her. Maybe that's why she embraced the costumes and makeup of the goth culture so much, spices to flavor a bland soup. She didn't dwell on her looks, and she pretended not to give a shit about what people thought of her, but I always felt that her apathy was a lie.

I'm an attractive girl, I know that, and I don't try to pretend like I'm not. I've been blessed with clear skin, straight teeth, good eyesight, good hair, an overactive metabolism—just plain great genetics. But, like Mel, I yearned for something different than hanging out with the cheerleaders at school. I had played the role of the perfect child growing up; I was a Girl Scout and took gymnastics all through middle school. I'm no genius, but I got all A's and B's in school—it just seemed to come easy to me. It was like a simple formula to follow—as long as you paid attention and read the assignments, the answers were all there in the work. My parents weren't as satisfied with my grades as I was. My father was always telling me that I wasn't going to get an academic scholarship to college. He warned me that I would have to work my way through college or get a student loan. Unlike Mel's parents, mine weren't busting at the seams with money and they constantly reminded me of that fact. They just assumed I was headed for college after high school, but I often informed them that college was no guarantee of a good job anymore—there were too many kids with degrees fighting for the few open job slots. I had no idea what I wanted to do with my life. I wanted my parents to let me be free for a few years and express myself, find myself, like Mel's parents were letting her do. My mom and dad weren't happy about my fascination with the counterculture world of darkness (probably how they thought of it), and the idea that I was hurting them in some small way gave me a little bit of pleasure, even though I didn't understand why.

I could see by then that they had given up on me and were focusing their attention on my two younger sisters, one in gymnastics and the other in cheerleading—just like me at that age. Maybe my parents were going back to the drawing board with my sisters, learning from the mistakes they felt they had made with me. Sometimes I felt paranoid, like the four of them were forming some cabal and conspiring against me, looking at me with pity like I was the lost one.

I loved my sisters, don't get me wrong. I still do. And they love me. But I believe you can love someone and still not like them very much, or find common ground.

I felt restless, like I was searching for something in life, but I didn't know what it was. I craved discovery and adventure. I craved danger—but only to a degree. I craved sensation and exploration. I craved darker things. My interest in the goth world wasn't just to go along with Mel's fascination with it—my interest was in the darker side of reality. I had started reading horror books and watching horror films. I had fantasies of dark sensual acts. I was looking for a dark knight on a black horse to lead me deeper into that world, and I found him that night at the house party.

Damon was tall and lean, not an ounce of fat on him. He was maybe a little too thin, but he was muscular with beautiful lines of veins bulging in his forearms. His dark hair came down to his shoulders, curling just a little at the ends. That night he had his hair tied back in a ponytail. His face was long and sculpted with sharp angles, like a dark hero from a graphic novel. His black pupils contrasted with his pale skin. His smile was seductive, and his canine teeth looked a little sharper than they should've been. He wore black jeans held up by a belt with a chain hanging from it, a black T-shirt, and biker boots. There was something in his stare, something in those watchful eyes, a hint of amusement in them as he looked at me like he was keeping a secret.

An hour later we were alone. We had drifted outside, away from the other partiers. We moved to a far corner of the backyard, hiding in the shadows. It was October, a few weeks away from Halloween, and the air was chilly for northern Florida at that time of year. We talked and it felt like we'd known each other for a long time. I felt at ease, yet nervous at the same time.

I could tell that Mel wasn't happy when she found us in the backyard. I'm sure she'd had her eye on Damon as soon as we had arrived, as I'm sure most of the girls there had. Mel didn't say anything on the way home about the time I'd spent with Damon. She talked about anything else but that. But I swore I could feel the anger coming off of her like heat from an oven. I could sense injustice fuming inside of her; the embers of jealousy that had always been there were flaring up at my assault into her lifestyle and her world.

FIVE

THERON

"That's when you and Damon got together?" Theron asked Cyn.

She stubbed out her cigarette into the plastic bowl and lit another. She took a sip from her can of Coke. "I couldn't keep away from him after that night."

"Did he go to your school?"

"He dropped out of high school when he was seventeen. He still lived with his mom. He didn't have a job, but he always seemed to have money."

"He dealt drugs," Theron said. It wasn't a question. He jotted down a few notes about Damon as she spoke.

"Some pot and pills. That's all I'd ever seen. He might have dealt a little meth, but he never admitted it. He didn't do any drugs and he never drank. He said he wanted his mind clear; he wanted to always be in control of his mind and body. Dealing drugs was just a business for him, just a way to make fast money without becoming one of the cattle at some dead-end job."

"Cattle?"

Cyn smiled. "He called most people cattle. He said most people were mindless cattle being herded here and there by their masters, and they never even knew it. In the beginning I thought he was talking about some deep-state government or new world order, but I would learn later that he meant something else entirely. He was talking about vampires."

"Vampires," Theron repeated.

"Damon was fascinated with vampires. He said he'd been obsessed with them since he was very young. He was drawn to the darker side of things, but vampires in particular. I wanted to experience those darker things with him. It was like he was putting out these pheromones and I was picking them up, some signal that only I could hone in on. I was willing right then to go to the darkest places with him, anywhere with him."

Cyn paused for a moment, hesitating. She sipped her Coke like her mouth had suddenly gone dry. She glanced back at the glass door of the office. The blinds over the windows were drawn, but parted just enough to let the orange glow of the streetlights in through the glass.

"But you didn't go to these dark places with him, did you?" Theron said. "That's why you contacted me. It's why you need help."

Cyn didn't answer.

"What did Damon do? You said you were afraid he was going to kill someone. You said something about a first kill."

Cyn still didn't answer. She glanced back at the glass door of the office. The drizzling rain had stopped but everything was still wet.

"We're okay," Theron said. "If anyone comes here, I've got my .45 on me." He touched the gun tucked into his shoulder holster. "I've also got a shotgun in the back room."

She looked back at him, but she didn't say anything for a moment.

Theron wondered if he had pushed Cyn too quickly with his barrage of questions. He needed to sit back and let her tell her story the way she wanted to.

Cyn finally started talking again. "I was a virgin when I met Damon. He was my first. My only. He opened up this dark world to me, and I fell hard for him. I was enthralled with him, infatuated with him. If he had a love of vampires, then I was willing to love them. If he believed in anarchy and revolutions, if he believed that society would eventually collapse, then I was willing to go along with it just to be with him."

"But things went too far, didn't they?"

Cyn didn't answer for a moment. She looked down at her hands, fiddling with her fingers. "Yes. They went too far."

#

CYN

Ever since we had met at that house party all those months ago, Damon and I had been together and we were growing closer every day. I was still friends with Mel, but our relationship had a slight strain to it after Damon and I were together. I still went out of my way to talk with Mel, to hang out with her. I even risked making Damon angry by spending more time with Mel. But no matter what I did, it just felt like Mel and I weren't as close as we used to be, like we would never be that close again.

Damon had his own friends, too. He had a lot of acquaintances, but he only had two really close friends: Jeremy Shaw and Ronnie Costas. Jeremy was Damon's age, and I'm sure he helped Damon with his drug dealing business since Jeremy never seemed to have a job either. He was the poorest of all five of us. His dad took off when Jeremy and his older brother were little, and Jeremy and his mom still live in a rundown trailer park on the south side of town. His mom used to be a stripper, but she was so strung out these days she couldn't even do that anymore. Jeremy was a few inches shorter than Damon, but he was stockier and muscular. He buzzed his hair short and seemed more like a punk than a goth, yet he complemented Damon somehow. They'd known each other since grade school, and they were both social outcasts in their own ways. But they always had each other's back.

Jeremy was a natural athlete. His brother went to college on some kind of athletic scholarship, but blew the whole thing by drinking and getting into trouble. Jeremy didn't even get that far—he failed high school because he'd rather spend his time drinking, smoking pot, and getting into trouble. It was a shame to see the potential he had wasted, but Damon said that Jeremy's freedom to make his own choice in life was his utmost prized possession, one that had to be cherished and defended. Damon said most people were cattle that followed the rules and lived in fear of stepping out of line, but Jeremy was truly free. Speeches like that from Damon fired Jeremy up and gave him an excuse for his anarchy and self-destruction. I always wondered what different path Jeremy might have taken in life if Damon hadn't planted those seeds in his mind.

Ronnie was two years older than Damon and Jeremy, twenty-one years old at the time I first met him, but he managed to both look and seem younger than the two of them. He was shorter than both of them and painfully thin. He had bouts of acne on his face and shoulders, and he wore thick glasses. Like Jeremy, Ronnie wasn't as much into the goth and vampire culture as Damon and Mel were, but he seemed to love Damon's views about society and anarchy even though he was one of the cattle, working a fulltime job as a forklift operator at a distribution center for some big box store. Somehow Ronnie managed to work a full week yet still have the energy to party all night with us. I don't know when he had time to sleep. But it didn't look like Ronnie slept much, anyway. He always seemed drained when he was around Damon and Jeremy, almost as if they sucked the energy out of him. I suspected that Ronnie was popping pills to stay awake, pills that he probably bought from Damon.

Ronnie lived in an apartment with his Uncle Stan. When his uncle was gone on a drinking binge, we'd go hang out there sometimes. The apartment was over the top of a large garage at a house that had been split up into apartments. Ronnie slept in the one bedroom in the apartment and his uncle slept on the couch.

There were other places where we hung out: the cemetery, parking lots, at Jeremy's trailer if his mother was out all night. Sometimes we went to clubs. We'd go down to the goth clubs in Tampa and St. Petersburg. And there was another club we went to up in Ocala. But the place where we spent the most time was an abandoned house that Damon had found. The house was way out on Allen Road, set far back from the road and hidden by trees and bushes. There was no water or electricity there, but we cleaned the place up and fixed the doors, installing new locks on them. No one ever came out there, and we made it our own.

Sometimes Damon and I just spent time together. He would take me for long rides on his motorcycle. And sometimes Damon and I just spent the night alone in his bedroom. We usually got a motel room outside of town once or twice a month just to have some time to ourselves. Those were the times I liked the best, when we were alone.

As the months went on, Damon and I grew closer. For a man who tried to show the world a hard and dangerous edge, he could be so sensitive when we were alone. We talked a lot. Damon had complex opinions about everything: society, the afterlife, fantasy, the supernatural, and of course, his favorite subject, vampires.

Damon had no real plans in life, and I liked that. My whole life had been planned out by my parents as soon as I was born. I never realized how much the thought of those plans had stressed me out. Being with Damon was like taking a break from all of that, like floating in limbo for a while, taking a break from life yet finally living for once.

It was a great nine months of bliss—parties, sex, travel, conversation, fantasizing. Damon turned me on in so many ways, not just sexually but intellectually. Damon introduced me to vampire books, but also to books about philosophy and history. I don't know if I'd really call Damon a goth like Mel was, his tastes went far deeper than just wearing some dark clothes and having piercings and tattoos. I was mesmerized by Damon's wildness and his freedom.

Even though Damon claimed to not have any goals or ambitions in his life, I couldn't help sensing that he was waiting for something big to come his way; there was this confidence that he was on a path and something great was waiting for him just down the road, something he was meant for. He seemed to be hiding a secret from me and everyone else. There was something in his smile and the way he looked at me. He knew, and had the rest of us convinced, that something life-altering and profound was coming for us. All we had to do was sit back and wait.

And then the very thing Damon had been waiting for came along—the Vampire Game.

SEVEN

THERON

Cyn stopped talking and lit another cigarette. She checked to see how many she had left in the pack.

Theron got up and went to the back room to grab two more cans of Coke. He came back out and set one down in front of Cyn, then he sat back down behind his desk. He opened his can of soda and took a long swallow. He still had the notebook and pen on the desk in front of him, a few pages of notes jotted down in his large, scrawling handwriting.

"What's the Vampire Game?" Theron asked.

"Damon had mentioned the Vampire Game a few times when he talked about the cabal of vampires that ruled the world. A lot of people thought the game was a myth, but Damon believed in it."

"Vampires rule the world?" Theron asked.

"Damon believed that. He said that vampires have been behind the scenes in positions of power, helping to secretly run the world for centuries, and they had plans to reveal themselves and take over the world soon. They didn't recruit often, but sometimes they did—through the Vampire Game. As the population of the world grew, they also needed to grow in numbers to keep pace. But recruitments to the Vampire Game weren't random; they only sent invitations to certain people, people they had been watching."

"And Damon believed he was being watched by them?"

"Yes. He told me that vampires were at the clubs, lurking in the shadows, blending in with the others. But they were always watching, always monitoring."

"Did you ever see any of these vampires?"

"Not then. But I've seen them in the last few weeks." She stared right at Theron. "And you've seen them, too. You saw one tonight."

Theron wasn't ready to admit that he had seen a vampire standing in the rain at the edge of a Dairy Queen parking lot. "What about Damon? Did you ever see him talk to any of the people he thought were vampires?"

Cyn shook her head no. "Like I said, I never saw any of them until recently."

Theron backed off for a moment, feeling like he might be pushing Cyn too much again. He sipped his Coke, replacing the need to sip a mixed drink with the sugary beverage, replacing one vice for another, and probably not a healthier one.

"When did Damon get an invitation to the Vampire Game?" Theron asked Cyn.

"About two months ago. In the middle of August."

"And that's when everything started happening?"

"Yes. That's when it all changed."

#

CYN

Damon called me on a Saturday morning, waking me up. He never usually called in the morning, but he was excited. He wanted all of us to meet at the abandoned house at sunset; he wanted to make sure none of us made any other plans for the night. He told me he would come by and get me around seven o'clock. He had some exciting news for all of us. I begged him to just tell me, but he wouldn't; he wanted all of us together first.

He came by at seven o'clock on the nose. I got on the back of his bike and held on to him as we rode to the abandoned house. The sun was setting by then, the day dying on the horizon in a blaze of crimson. It felt chilly even though it was still the summer and hot as hell. But on the back of Damon's bike, and with the night coming, and with the anticipation of this big news that Damon was so excited about, I felt myself shivering.

"They sent me an invitation to the Vampire Game," Damon said when we had all gathered inside the living room of the house. We had a few battery-powered lanterns in the house, but we only used candles that night, sitting in a circle on the floor around a collection of lit candles. Jeremy had already started drinking from a bottle of vodka. He had his shirt off as usual.

"What's the Vampire Game?" Ronnie asked.

"It's a game that will help us become vampires," Damon said. He flipped through his cell phone to a screen and then showed each of us.

I was the last one to look at Damon's phone. On the screen was a webpage with a black background. The words THE VAMPIRE GAME were scrawled at the top of the page in a fancy script. There was a pair of woman's red lips below that with fangs and a few drops of blood dripping from them. At the bottom of the page was a rectangle with the words ENTER CODE right above it.

I handed Damon's phone back to him.

"They sent the code to me," Damon said. "It's in a text. I'll show it to you."

I'd never seen Damon so giddy. It was the first time that I could imagine him as a child—he seemed like an eight-year-old boy at that moment, a boy who had just unwrapped a Christmas present and gotten exactly what he had wished for. And I guess he *had* gotten exactly what he had desired most in his life—an invitation to the game.

"Is this like an RPG?" Mel asked.

"No," Damon told her. "This isn't a role-playing game. This is real. This is a game that teaches you how to become a vampire, a step-by-step process."

We were all quiet for a moment, a sudden tension and wonder blanketing our circle. Even the candles seemed to flicker as if a ghost had just drifted over them. I watched the other three; they seemed to be looking away from Damon, almost like they were hesitant to meet his gaze, like they were struggling to hold on to reality and not fall down his rabbit hole of fantasy. Or maybe they were afraid of bursting his bubble, afraid one of them might have to deliver the bad news that he was being punked by some online game that wasn't real.

While everyone was quiet, Damon went into one of his speeches about the cabal of vampires. "Centuries ago a man found a tomb in Eastern Europe. The exact location is still a secret. The legend goes that the man found an opening in the side of a hill, guarded by stones, but he could tell it was definitely a tomb of some kind. The man was a poor farmer, and the first thing that came to his mind was that there could be treasure buried down there with the body. He recruited the help of his son, and they removed the stones and ventured down into the underground crypt. They found a coffin but no treasure. After prying the coffin lid loose, they discovered that there wasn't a body inside—it was just an empty coffin. The farmer wondered why someone would go to so much trouble to bury an empty coffin. As he placed the lid back onto the coffin, the farmer cut himself on a piece of metal he hadn't noticed before at the edge of the lid. He didn't know it then, but he had been infected with an ancient virus, a vampire virus that changed him fundamentally, changed him at the cellular level, and even at the genetic level. He became stronger, quicker, and smarter. His senses were heightened. His immune system went into overdrive, killing anything that could hurt him and preserving his body from aging. He found he could go for days without water and months without food—but there was one thing that he craved, blood."

Damon went on to explain that this man was the first that anyone knew of who had become an actual vampire, and that this man went on to rule his town, then his territory. He recruited others, using a process, a game of sorts, a series of tests so that he could trust the new recruits. Everything was done in secrecy, but once the recruits were vampires, they were part of a cabal that would go on to rule parts of the world.

"Don't vampires live forever?" Mel asked.

"That is a point of debate," Damon told her. "And maybe it's something all of us will find out once we have completed the tasks in the game. There are some who theorize that vampires age more slowly than humans, and their immunity to diseases and rapid healing of injuries keeps them healthy for centuries. Some theorize that vampires live one year for every ten or twenty years a human lives. Others say it might be more like one year for every fifty years, or even a hundred. No one knows for sure unless you are a vampire, unless you are part of that secret society."

"If vampires live forever, and they were ruling all of these places in the world, then how come they're not still in power?" Mel asked. It was a reasonable question, one I had myself.

"Some are still in power behind the scenes," Damon told her. He wasn't angry about Mel's questions. He was gentle with her, like he was teaching a class; he was patient with everyone's questions, even patient with anyone's obvious doubts. "The vampires stay in the background. They're the ones pulling the strings, the ones with the true power that no one knows about: counsel to royalty, secretaries to leaders and presidents, trusted men and women of emperors, leaders of companies and empires. They seem like they die off, even having fake funerals so others can take their place and not give away the secret of their longevity. But those ancient ones are still in the shadows, still helping to rule. They've been working on this for centuries, waiting for the opportunity for total control of the world—a new world order, only an order run by vampires. And now, with the technology we have today, they're so close."

"So you're saying everyone in power all over the world is a vampire?" Ronnie asked. He didn't seem to be challenging Damon; instead, he stared at Damon with a wide-eyed expression of wonder.

"Not everyone in power is a vampire," Damon said. "Not yet. But there are undoubtedly some vampires in positions of power right now, maybe not presidents and chancellors and prime ministers, nothing in the spotlight, but like I just said, they are in positions of power in the background, pulling the strings. These days they might be the CEO's of certain corporations, directors of intelligence agencies, secretaries of treasuries or presidents of central banks—the ones with the real power in this world, not the figureheads."

We were all silent for a moment. Damon had a way of making you believe, a way of drawing you into his world and infecting you with his passion.

"Have there been setbacks along the way?" Damon asked as if one of us had voiced the question. "Of course. Revolutions have occurred; royal families have been replaced with governing bodies, examples like the French Revolution and the American Revolution come to mind. The cabal had to change their tactics quickly; they had to change with the times. But as technology advanced, they saw a new way to attain power; they saw an Orwellian world of total global control. And we can be a part of that."

We were still silent.

"All by playing a game?" Jeremy asked.

We all laughed—except Damon. But he wasn't angry; again, he was patient. "It's more like a test—like completing a series of tasks."

The laughter died down and everyone was quiet for a moment.

"No one here has to play the game," Damon said. "I'm not forcing anyone to join. But you have to decide tonight. I can include a select few, and I have chosen the four of you. But it's your choice. The only thing is that if you decline tonight, you can't enter the game later."

Jeremy took a big swig from his bottle of vodka. "I'm in," he said.

Of course Jeremy was in; he would follow Damon to the gates of hell if he asked him to.

"Me too," Mel said.

Another of Damon's worshippers.

Ronnie looked slightly concerned, perhaps thinking about his daytime job that he protected so religiously. He was the only one of us who was possibly growing up a little, maybe because he was the only one who had lived past the age of twenty so far.

"What about you, Cyn?" Damon asked me. He stared at me, waiting for my answer.

I didn't answer him. I wasn't ready to commit just yet. I was as cautious as Ronnie was at that moment; I wanted to know more about the game before I punched a code into this Vampire Game. I couldn't help suspecting that there were things that Damon wasn't telling us, I couldn't help feeling that he was giving us all the good news and leaving out some of the bad news.

"What do we do in this game?" Ronnie asked. "How do we play?"

"We each enter a code that will be given to us by a text message," Damon said. "And then the game starts for all of us. After we complete our first task, we watch our phones for the next text message with the code for our next task."

"What kind of tasks?" Ronnie asked.

Damon shrugged. "I don't know yet. We won't know until we're in the game. But we need to complete each task together and within a certain period of time before we can move on to the next task. We'll all need to type in our code after each task is complete."

"What if we don't complete the task?" I asked.

"Then the game is over for that person," Damon answered. "That person doesn't get to become a vampire. But the others who completed the task can move on in the game." He looked at the others. "You have to remember, once you're out of the game, you're out for good." He looked back at me. "There are no second chances."

I felt a chill run through me then, like he was talking about more than just the game. "What if we lie?" I asked. "What if we say we did the task but didn't? What if we just enter the code anyway?"

Damon looked at me like I had blasphemed the game in some way. For an anarchist, Damon seemed to give a lot of weight to rules lately. "They will know," he told me.

"How?" I challenged.

Damon didn't answer.

I laughed. Maybe I was trying to pass all of this off as a joke. Maybe this was all getting a little too serious for me. "Are they watching us?"

"They're always watching," Damon said.

I wanted to laugh again—it was a natural reaction. But I didn't.

"You don't have to do this," Damon told me, but I could see the yearning in his eyes, the hope that I would agree to come along on this journey with him. But I could also see at that moment that Damon was willing to go without me. He was willing to walk away from me for a chance at this. I felt a surge of panic. I knew I loved Damon then, but I suddenly doubted that he loved me as strongly. I felt at that moment that I was competing with a mistress, the lure of this dark world that he would always love more than me or anyone else. And to prove to Damon—and his mistress—my love, I agreed to play the game.

Now it was Ronnie's turn to commit.

Damon was happy now that I had agreed to play. I could see it on his face; Damon was thrilled that his girlfriend and his best friend Jeremy were joining him. I couldn't help feeling that he looked at Mel and Ronnie as extras. I knew he would love to have all five of us together in the game, but he would sacrifice those two for me and Jeremy in a second if he had to. I knew it then.

"Think of what it would be like to be a vampire," Damon told Ronnie, trying to convince him, but I believe he was really talking to all of us, trying to close the deal before any of us changed our minds. "Think of the freedom. The power. You could live forever, young and strong and powerful. And rich."

"Rich?" Ronnie asked.

Damon nodded—he had found Ronnie's trigger. "Oh, I forgot to mention. Along with the tasks in the game, there are rewards along the way."

"What kind of rewards?" Ronnie asked.

"I don't know," Damon answered. "I don't know what the rewards are any more than I know what the tasks are. We have to play the game to find out."

"Come on," Jeremy said, nudging Ronnie. "Grow a pair."

Ronnie snatched the bottle of vodka out of Jeremy's hand and chugged down a few swallows. He handed the bottle across the circle to Damon. "I'm in."

Damon took a small sip and passed the bottle to Mel. I could see the glee, even the hope, in her eyes because Damon had passed the bottle to her before me. She guzzled down some of the vodka, her face turning red almost immediately.

We were all in—we were all ready to begin the game.

NINE

THERON

"So that's how the game started?" Theron asked.

Cyn nodded.

"What did you guys do next?"

"We each downloaded the game onto our phones from the website that Damon showed us."

"What's the website?"

Cyn dug her phone out of her pocket and looked up the website. "I can give you the website address, but you have to go to the dark web to pull it up."

Theron nodded. He knew about the dark web.

She slid her phone across the desk to Theron. He had his own phone out and he looked up the website on his phone. When he found it, he compared his phone with Cyn's phone. The screen was the same on both phones, just a black background with the female bloody lips and vampire fangs, and the words THE VAMPIRE GAME above them. And there was the box below to enter the code.

"My code doesn't work anymore," Cyn said. "Once we downloaded the game, Damon gave us a code from his text message. He had a code for himself and a code for four other people, but like I said, that was just the entry code. It was almost like they knew how many people Damon would want to include with him in the game. There was a separate code for each of us, and we punched the codes into our phones right there in that house and then we were officially in the game."

"You got your first task then?" Theron asked. He moved his phone to the side of his desk and slid Cyn's phone back to her after jotting down the website address onto his notepad.

"Not then," she said as she slipped her phone back into her jacket pocket. "Damon said we would be notified by text and given a new code and a date and time of when the first task needed to be completed. We were supposed to keep an eye out for any texts coming in."

"You told me earlier on the phone that you talked to the police about this already."

"Not about the game."

"You never told the police about this game?"

"I told them about Damon and the things he started doing."

"Like what?"

"I'm getting to that. Besides, if I would have told them about the game, they never would have believed me about anything else."

"The police could've traced the texts on your phone."

"We were supposed to erase the texts after we got them."

"They could still trace them from the servers at the cell phone company."

Cyn shrugged. "They would need a warrant, wouldn't they? I thought a crime needed to be committed to get a warrant."

"So, you're saying no crimes have been committed yet?"

Cyn shook her head. "No, I'm not saying that. Crimes *have* been committed."

"Are you talking about this person Damon's going to kill?"

She shrugged. "All five of us committed crimes over these last two months. They were small crimes at first, and then they got worse and worse. I just can't prove the worst ones yet. That's why I need you."

Theron sat back and sighed. His office chair creaked a little.

"You don't believe me about this, do you?" Cyn asked.

Theron was a little shocked by the bluntness of her question . . . her accusation. "I believe *you* believe it. I believe your friends probably believe in this."

Cyn was quiet for a moment. She looked at the front door again like she was expecting Damon and his friends to show up at any moment. "I know you don't believe me, and you're really not going to believe me when I tell you the rest of it." She looked back at him. "But I swear it's all true."

"What was your first task?" Theron asked.

#

CYN

I got the text message the next day. I typed my code into the website and a new screen appeared with a task on it. The task was for all of us.

We met at the abandoned house. Damon brought a razor knife, a box of bandages, and a bottle of rubbing alcohol with him. I rode on the back of Damon's bike to the house that night, and the sunset reminded me of the evening before. But I had been in a different mood the night before—excited and hopeful. Tonight, I felt nervous about what we were going to do.

When we were all at the abandoned house, we sat in a circle on the floor, just like we'd done the night before. We collected some candles in the center of the circle and lit them. It was a windy night. I heard the tree branches and bushes blowing around outside. Some of the overgrown shrubs hugging the house scratched at the windows. It was like we had an audience of demons surrounding the house, watching us, waiting for us to perform our ritual and to begin our journey.

"We need to become brethren," Damon told us. "We need to become one. We need to share our blood."

I watched Damon as he sat across from me, his face seeming to shift slightly in the flickering candlelight. The rest of the house was hidden in darkness all around us.

"I just put a brand new blade in here," Damon said, indicating the razor knife in his hand, the kind you would cut carpet or drywall with. The little triangle of sharp steel poked out of the metal handle and the candlelight winked off the point of the blade. Damon held the razorblade over the flickering candle for thirty seconds to sterilize it.

We were supposed to cut our thumbs and then mix our blood with everyone else's. I'd heard of the whole blood brother thing before, a child's game, but I'd never done it before. Maybe young boys did this kind of thing out in the boonies somewhere, but I had never known anyone who had tried it.

When the knife was passed to me, I hesitated for just a moment, feeling sick to my stomach. I felt like this was a gruesome act to ask of us—and this was only the first task; I could only imagine what the next tasks were going to be. I worried about diseases, and even mentioned it before we started passing the knife around. I didn't want to hurt anyone's feelings—I trusted Damon and Mel, but I was a little suspicious of Jeremy and Ronnie's blood.

"I'm clean," Jeremy said with a grin when I voiced my concern about HIV or hepatitis. He shoved Ronnie playfully. "And you don't have to worry about Ronnie, he's still a virgin."

"No I'm not," Ronnie said, but he blushed in the candlelight.

"I'm not worried," Mel said. She seemed to take every opportunity to show her willingness to serve Damon and to upstage me at every turn, to prove how devoted she was not only to this game, but to Damon.

"It will be fine," Damon said, staring at me. "When we're finally vampires, there won't be a disease in the world that can hurt us."

They were all waiting on me to begin.

Damon scooted right up next to me and gently took the razor knife from my hands. "Let me do this," he said to me in a low, sultry voice as he took my left hand in his and caressed my thumb. "Look away," he whispered. "You won't feel a thing."

I let him take my hand, and for a few seconds I imagined we were playing some kind of dark erotic game. I felt a sharp pinch on my thumb. I looked back and Damon was already pressing a piece of gauze against the wound. "Hold it there for a few seconds until all of us are ready," he told me. "Keep pressure on it."

Damon sliced his thumb without hesitation—he didn't even wince. He handed the razor knife to Jeremy.

When everyone had sliced their thumbs, we rubbed our bloody wounds together. I rubbed mine with Damon and Mel, then Jeremy and Ronnie. Afterwards, we rinsed our cuts with rubbing alcohol and smeared some antibacterial cream on them, then covered them with a Band-Aid.

We were done. We were siblings by blood. We were family. We were one.

ELEVEN

THERON

"What was your next task?" Theron asked Cyn.

"The next task came about a week later. My cut had healed up by then. I was worried about it getting infected, but it was fine. I was worried about getting some kind of blood disease, especially from Jeremy. I believed that Ronnie really might be a virgin. Of course that would change soon—Mel would eventually offer herself to him, and then to Jeremy. She felt that we should share not only our blood, but our bodies."

Theron arched his eyebrows in surprise.

"I didn't feel that way," Cyn said quickly. "I was only with Damon, and he was only with me at that time, no matter how badly Mel wanted him. I know Mel was trying to work her way to Damon, figuring that she could use the Vampire Game as the excuse, but Damon must have politely refused her advances, or let her know in some way that he wasn't going to cheat on me."

"And you still believe that he was truthful with you about everything? Even now?"

"Damon was always honest with me. But everything *has* changed in these last two weeks. I don't know the truth anymore."

The intensity with which Cyn still defended Damon, even with everything that had happened, surprised Theron. He knew when to back off; he didn't want to make her angry.

"So you were blood brothers and sisters," Theron said. "What was your second task?"

TWELVE

CYN

For our second task we decided to all meet at Ronnie's apartment since his uncle would be gone for the night, hitting the bars like he did a few nights a week until his disability check ran out halfway through the month.

Damon bought a raw steak at the supermarket and brought it to Ronnie's house. I had ridden there with Mel and Jeremy. We sat around the small table in Ronnie's kitchen and Damon laid the meat wrapped in butcher paper on the table and then opened it.

We were all supposed to eat a piece of raw meat. I know it doesn't sound like a particularly challenging task, but I still didn't want to do it. I wasn't a vegan by any stretch, but I liked the meat I ate to be cooked; I didn't even like rare steak, and I sure as hell never tried sushi.

The others seemed fine with eating raw meat. Damon used a steak knife from Ronnie's kitchen drawer to cut the meat into smaller pieces, but I made Damon wash the knife first. I didn't care if I was hurting Ronnie's feelings or not, his apartment was a pig sty.

When I read what our challenge was on the website, I insisted on using steak because I'd read somewhere that it was the safest meat to eat raw. Chicken could have salmonella and raw pork was out of the question. And raw fish didn't feel right—this task seemed like it had to be some kind of mammal flesh.

"Some people eat steak tartare," Damon joked when he saw my expression.

I stared down at the slab of meat, not bothering to look at him. "Let's just get this over with."

Damon cut smaller chunks of meat for all of us and put them on paper plates, one for each of us. I used the steak knife to cut my chunk of meat into even smaller pieces.

I ate a small piece of the meat at the same time as the others. The meat was rubbery and bloody. It seemed to take forever to chew it. I finally swallowed the lump of meat and washed it down with some of my bottled water, and then I started on the next piece of meat.

Jeremy was the first one finished. It seemed like he had barely chewed the meat, just swallowing it down like a big dog wolfing down a treat. When he was done, he cut off another hunk of meat to eat.

"You don't get extra brownie points for eating more of it," I told him.

He flipped me a bird. "I like it," he said, smiling at me and shoving another hunk of the raw meat into his mouth.

Mel cut off another piece of meat for herself, trying to keep up with Jeremy like this was some kind of drinking game.

"We should drink the blood, too," Jeremy said, nearly frothing with excitement. He got a plastic bowl from the cabinet and then carefully emptied the blood puddled on the butcher paper into the bowl. I didn't make Jeremy wash the bowl out because I had no intention of sipping the blood in it.

But when the bowl was passed to me, I locked eyes with Damon. He stared at me with a strange expression; there was amusement in his eyes. He seemed curious about what I was going to do, curious about how enthusiastic I was going to be. But I swore I also saw doubt in his eyes, and suddenly I wanted to challenge his presumptions about me. I wanted to shock him so I sipped the blood, feeling like I had proven myself to him and the others.

After we were done, Jeremy broke out his small bottle of vodka, and he and Ronnie started drinking.

I felt strange as I sat there at the small table. I didn't feel like a vampire, but I also felt a sense of comradery with the others, like even though what we had just done was mundane, it still felt like we had all gone through something together. I'd had the same feeling as a girl on the gymnastics team—I felt like a part of something with them at that time, and I felt like a part of something now with Damon, Mel, Jeremy, and Ronnie.

An hour later Jeremy caught a ride home with Mel, and I rode on the back of Damon's bike. He drove me to a little wooded area near the river where we liked to hang out sometimes; it was our own secret little place. We kissed and made out for a little bit under the starlight.

"Jeremy and Mel are sleeping together," I told Damon after we stopped kissing.

He just smiled and nodded. He already knew, of course. Maybe he and Jeremy talked about us like me and Mel talked about them.

Damon wanted to kiss some more—he wanted our kissing to lead to something else. But I wasn't in the mood. I still felt weird, like I had this fog of malaise hanging over me.

"Why a piece of raw meat?" I asked him.

Damon just shrugged. If he was upset that I had rejected his sexual advances, he didn't act like it. He was still smiling, still looking at me like something about me amused him.

"I mean, I understand about the whole blood brother thing," I told him, "but not the meat."

"I think they want us to get used to the taste of blood," he said.

His words sent a chill through me, and I felt a panicky feeling that I'd already gotten too deep into something dangerous, and that if I went too much deeper I wasn't going to be able to escape. I had been thinking of this whole thing as a game—it was called the Vampire Game. But I knew Damon was taking it very seriously. He wanted so badly to believe this was all real. I worried that when he found out the truth, that this was just some sick game to see how far some gullible vampire wannabes would go, he would be crushed. I wondered how he was going to take it after investing all of his belief into this. How far would he go in this game? It was the first time I began to worry about Damon's sanity. Of course I was still in love with him, but I wished there was a way I could protect him from this game, a way to cushion his fall when it inevitably came.

They want us to get used to the taste of blood. Damon's words echoed in my mind. Were we really going to eventually drink blood? Human blood? Was that what all of this was really leading up to?

The rational part of my mind took over. It was just a game, I told myself. Besides, if it got too crazy, I could always quit. Damon wouldn't like me quitting, but I had my limits. I loved Damon, but if it went too far . . . well, surely he would recognize that point, wouldn't he? He would be able to tell if things were going too far.

As if Damon could sense my concerns, he did his best to soothe my worries that night. And thirty minutes later I felt a little better.

Damon drove me home. My parents were angry because I had stayed out past my curfew on a school night. I'd only broken my curfew by forty-five minutes, but they were still mad. Their anger had more to do with *who* I had stayed out late with rather than how long I had stayed out. They saw a demon out there on that motorcycle, a demon who was slowly taking their child away from them. If they'd only known more of the story, if they had known how bad things were going to get, I think they would've stepped in sooner.

THIRTEEN

THERON

"Okay," Theron said. "Your first task was to become blood brothers. And blood sisters. Your next task was to eat raw meat. What did you have to do after that?"

"At least a week passed before we got our next two tasks—two of them back to back. Just when I had begun feeling comfortable again, beginning to forget about the game, just when things between me and Damon began to feel normal again, I got a text message to enter my new code into the website."

"What kind of code did you get for each task?" Theron asked with his pen poised over his notepad.

"It was just a series of random numbers and letters. Kind of like a password or something."

Theron nodded for her to continue with her story.

"I dreaded the new task that was coming, fearing the worst before I even knew what it was. At that time I imagined a group of computer nerds somewhere watching the game, controlling it, coming up with the craziest and most disgusting things they could think of for us to do. I imagined them smoking a joint and laughing hysterically every time we let them know we had completed the latest task. I never believed for a second that any of the game was true. I was just going along with it because Damon wanted to believe so badly."

Cyn stopped talking for a moment. She lit another cigarette, her hands trembling slightly.

To Theron, Cyn looked older than her eighteen years at that moment. "What was your next task?" Theron prodded, trying to keep her talking.

"We had to destroy something that was personal to us."

Theron just nodded.

"I chose a ring my mother had given to me on my sixteenth birthday, some old-fashioned thing that her grandmother had passed down to her. I'm sure it was expensive, but I wasn't really that in love with it. But it meant a lot to my mother—that's why I chose to destroy it."

Cyn stopped talking.

Theron watched her in the darkness, but he could tell that she was struggling to hold back tears.

"I shouldn't have done it," she whispered. "If I could go back in time and change things . . ." She let her words hang in the air and inhaled deeply on the cigarette.

The smell of the cigarette smoke was getting to Theron again, tempting him, but he didn't want to say anything to her about it.

"We met at the abandoned house. We were in the living room. When it was my turn, I took the ring out of my pocket and laid it on the wood floor. I brought a hammer with me. For just a few seconds I hesitated after I lifted the hammer up. I wanted to quit the game right then and there. I even asked Damon what kind of game would want us to do something like this. He explained that they wanted us to turn our backs on our possessions, on the things that meant anything to us, to renounce our world so we could enter theirs. So I destroyed it. I smashed the ring flat with the hammer. I hit it again and again."

Cyn was quiet for a moment.

"What did you do with it after that?"

"I threw it away. Threw it in the weeds behind the house. I never told my mother. She still doesn't know." She stared right at Theron. "And I don't want her to know."

Theron nodded. "Of course not."

Cyn inhaled a final drag of her cigarette then exhaled smoke as she stubbed it out in the plastic bowl on the desk.

"I can't even remember what the others sacrificed," Cyn said. "I think Ronnie busted some kind of whiskey glass his uncle had saved all these years, something he'd gotten when he was in the military or something. And Mel destroyed something of her brother's. I can't even remember what Jeremy brought. Damon, he had something of his father's—one of the few things he had from him, some kind of toy or something, a gift from his father that he had saved for years. But Damon said he was ready to banish the memories of his father. His father had never returned after Damon turned three years old; he could barely remember him now, and he didn't want to remember him at all. If his father didn't want to see him, then Damon said he didn't want anything to do with him."

"What happened next?"

"We all entered our codes to show that the task was complete. We got the next task the next day, and they didn't give us a lot of time to complete it."

"What was your next task?"

FOURTEEN

CYN

They wanted us to steal something. Like the items we were told to destroy, whatever we stole had to have some value to someone, and the item had to mean something to the person we were stealing it from. The other stipulation was that we had to steal from a stranger—we couldn't steal something from someone we knew.

We didn't have a lot of time to complete the task. Jeremy and Ronnie finished their tasks right away. Jeremy lifted a man's wallet when he wasn't looking and Ronnie stole someone's cell phone from an unlocked car. Mel stole something from a department store. I asked Damon if he would be my lookout. Of course he said yes, anything to help me complete the task.

Damon drove me into town. We rode up and down the main streets, past the lines of shops and stores, the government buildings, the parks. I rode on the back of his bike with my arms wrapped around him, trying to think of what I could steal. I didn't want to steal from a store, I wasn't quite that brave. I was sure that I would grab something, run, and then be caught immediately.

But then I saw it. I squeezed Damon's waist, my signal for him to pull over. He turned into a parking lot and parked his bike, shutting it off. He turned and looked at me.

"You know what you want to do?" he asked.

I nodded. I'd just seen a woman waiting at a bus stop. She was sitting by herself on a bench, and she had her purse on the bench seat next to her. She was reading a paperback book while she waited for the bus. I figured her interest in the book could be enough of a distraction while I grabbed her purse, but I asked Damon if he would create a diversion, just to be sure. He agreed immediately.

My heart was thumping as I walked down the sidewalk towards the bench where the lady waited. The bus stop sign was right beside her, but the city bus was nowhere in sight.

Damon was already way ahead of me. He walked a few feet past the woman and was about to step out into the street as cars and trucks approached. The woman jumped to her feet, yelling at him to watch out for the traffic.

This was my chance. I swooped in towards the bench and picked up the purse.

Damon had turned to the lady, smiling at her, never looking my way once as I walked away, slipping the purse over my shoulder. Damon had the woman hypnotized with his smile and his eyes as he thanked her. The woman was older, maybe in her forties. She was a little overweight, her graying hair pulled back into a bun. She wore some kind of uniform, like she was a maid in a motel or maybe a housekeeper. I couldn't tell where she worked and I didn't really care; I just wanted to get this over with.

I went around the block, doing my best not to run. I felt like every eye from the buildings and businesses were on me. I expected someone to shout, "Stop, thief!" But no one ever did.

A few minutes later I was back in the parking lot, entering it from the next street over, but Damon wasn't there yet. I was panicking for a moment, thinking someone had seen us and knew we had worked together to steal that woman's purse. I imagined cops were already at the scene, detaining Damon. I was tempted to walk to the parking lot's other entrance and look down the sidewalk. I was just about to do that, but then Damon came strolling up with a smile.

"Where were you?" I asked, shouting at him without meaning to.

"I was trying to help that poor lady look for the criminal that stole her purse."

I tried not to laugh. I didn't want to laugh, but the whole situation seemed absurd. What kept me from laughing was Damon's glee in what we had just done.

"Let's just go," I told him.

"Nobody's going to catch us," he said as he got on his bike. "We were meant for this." He started his bike and we sped away.

We were supposed to meet at the abandoned house later that afternoon. Damon and I got there before any of the others. He wanted to see if we had scored anything inside the lady's purse. We sat at the table and I dumped the contents out of the purse: she had a wallet, some tissues, a bottle of pills, a pack of gum, a tiny bottle of perfume, an extra Maxi-pad, an inhaler, her bus pass, and a few other odds and ends.

"Maybe you can sell these," I told Damon as I handed him the bottle of pills.

He read the label and shook his head. "No. These are prescription pills for something." He was already on his cell phone looking up the name of the medicine. "It's for anti-anxiety. And the inhaler's for asthma."

I felt my heart drop. I pictured the woman freaking out without her medication and inhaler, maybe hyperventilating and having a panic attack.

I went through her wallet. She had some money in there, which Damon told me to keep—he told me that I had earned it. Fifty-six dollars. Not much, but judging by the woman's appearance, and the fact that she needed to take the bus to work, it might have been a fortune to her.

The bus pass laid there off to the side. I picked it up and looked at it. It was some kind of card that was laminated with a bar code on one edge. I guessed it was something the woman might have paid for weekly or monthly from her bank card or something. I realized then that she probably couldn't have gotten on the bus without the pass. She'd been dressed for work, some kind of maid or housekeeper. I wondered if she'd been late for work. I wondered if she worked for a dickhead boss who told her if she was late one more time she would be fired. I wondered if she'd been fired. She'd lost a lot of her money, her photos of her kids, so many of her possessions. She was probably freaking out, she probably needed those anti-anxiety meds and her inhaler right now more than ever.

I felt bad. I know I wasn't supposed to feel that way—that was the point of this task, to disassociate ourselves from the cattle that we would eventually be feeding on, at least that's how Damon interpreted it. But I couldn't help feeling bad for what I had done. I had been responsible for maybe one of the worst days in this woman's life.

FIFTEEN

THERON

id you tell Damon how you felt?" Theron asked Cyn.

She shook her head no.

"Was that when you wanted out of the game?"

"I think it was the beginning of it. I had never really committed a crime like that before. I'd done some partying and skipping school, but I'd never stolen anything before. I didn't think it was really a big deal at first. I was more worried about getting busted than what I was actually doing. But after seeing the woman's stuff in her purse, the photos of her kids, the bus pass, her medication and inhaler, I realized that I had really hurt this person just by taking her purse. I just wish I would've stolen something from a store like Mel had done."

"So you completed these two tasks back to back," Theron said.

"Yeah."

"Then it was a while before you had to do another task?"

"We got a reward first."

"A reward?"

"Yeah. Remember I told you that Damon said we would get some rewards along the way. I guess we got them after reaching a certain milestone or something. Actually, this was our second reward."

"Your second one?"

"Yeah. I forgot to tell you about the first one. After we had completed the first two tasks, Damon was sent a text with the account number for our reward."

"Like an account number to a bank?"

"Yeah. A bank downtown. One of the big banking chains. Someone had opened an account there and deposited a thousand dollars into it. Jeremy and Ronnie wanted to spend the money right away, but Damon talked them into waiting. He told them that the money was proof that the vampires were real and that we were doing just fine in the game. But he also thought the money might be a test to see how disciplined we were, another test to turn our backs on our world. 'You don't get anything for free,' he told all of us."

"And you don't think—"

"Yeah," she said, nodding. "I already know what you're going to say: Damon opened the account on his own so he could make it look like the vampires had given us a reward."

Theron sat back, his leather office chair creaking just a bit. That was exactly what he was going to suggest. He figured Damon had probably used some of his drug dealing money to open the account and that was why he didn't want his friends spending it.

"I thought of that, too," she said. "I was pretty sure he had deposited the money into that account, but after we got our second reward, I wasn't so sure anymore. When we got our second reward, I was starting to believe that all of this could be real."

"What was your second reward?"

"We were invited to a party."

"A party?"

"Yes . . . a vampire party."

SIXTEEN

CYN

The party was at a mansion on the bay somewhere south of Tampa. I don't really remember where it was; Mel drove us that night in her minivan and I hadn't really paid attention to how we'd gotten there.

Before we left for the party, we printed out our invitations to take with us. The instructions given along with this reward stipulated that we had to have our invitations with us to get into the party. Along with that instruction, we were also told that the party would have a gothic theme and to dress accordingly. It was also a masquerade party and we would all need to wear masks.

We stopped at a party supply store along the way and bought Mardi Gras masks. Of course Jeremy had to be the oddball and he brought a rubber Captain America mask with him that was just slightly too large for his head, the edges of it flapping at his skin around the lower half of his face.

I wore a pair of tight black leather pants that Damon loved to see me in, a pair of high heeled boots, a black sleeveless top, and lace, fingerless opera gloves. I wore my leather bands, bracelets, silver jewelry and rings. Mel helped me with my makeup and hair, and I helped her pick out some clothes—a revealing short black dress that hugged her curvaceous body. The boys wore dark pants and biker boots, black T-shirts. Damon wore a long black trench coat with the collar turned up.

Jeremy brought a bottle of vodka, already sipping from it on the way there. Damon warned him not to get too drunk before we got there. Damon knew this was a reward, but like the money in the bank account, he believed this was as much of a test as a treat. He believed that we would all be watched when we got to the party, studied by the vampires among the crowd, observed to see if we were what they wanted. Yes, we had completed the four tasks so far, but Damon believed the vampires wanted more than blind obedience; he believed they wanted us to willingly adopt their culture, to see it as superior to the dreary lives of humans.

Almost two hours later we arrived at a gated community. We stopped at the guard shack. Mel told the guard who we were visiting. He checked our names on a list fixed to a clipboard. It took a few moments, but he finally opened the gate for us.

The streets meandered through a neighborhood of mansions, each house built on acres of land. Some of the houses looked like the size of small apartment buildings to me. Lighted windows managed to look cozy in the night even though the sprawling mansions were the exact opposite of cozy.

Mel followed the winding road to the back of the neighborhood that hugged Tampa Bay. The houses by the water went from mansions to obscenities of wealth. Many of the homes had their own gates protecting the entrance to their driveways, and the mansion we were visiting was no different. Three men dressed in black and wearing sunglasses signaled Mel to stop her minivan in front of a massive metal gate. One man waited by the computer panel that controlled the gate while the other two men approached the van, one at the driver's side, and the other at the passenger side.

The guard on the driver's side motioned for Mel to roll down the window. We had all donned our masks. We were quiet, all of us holding our breath. Damon's words had infected us, and now we believed that the test had truly begun. We were so close, right at the threshold of the world we all wanted, and it was up to these gatekeepers to let us pass. I saw the mansion in the distance, built up close to the seawall along the shore of the bay. The house was a lighted beacon in contrast to the dark waters of the bay, a towering, three-story edifice with cars parked all over the front yard and driveway.

"Invitations," the guard said. Even though he was clothed from head to toe, I could tell he was two hundred and forty pounds of nothing but bone and muscle. He held out a meaty hand, waiting for our paperwork.

We handed our invitations to Mel and she handed them to the guard.

The guard shuffled through each invitation. I wasn't sure how he could read them in the dark with his sunglasses on, but he seemed to be studying them intently. His clothing didn't hide the sidearm holstered on his hip, the butt of the pistol poking out from that holster. His scrutiny of our invitations seemed to be taking forever.

After a few moments, the guard leaned in and looked at the rest of us as Mel shrank back from him. He stared at each one of us, but he looked at Jeremy the longest. "You can't wear that mask in there," he said in an emotionless voice, almost like a growl.

Jeremy yanked off the Captain America mask and dropped it on the floor of the van. Damon already had the extra Mardi Gras mask in his hand, giving it to Jeremy who slipped it on.

I was sure then that Jeremy had ruined it for all of us. We had been given simple instructions, and we had already proven that we couldn't follow them. Jeremy had to be different; he had to be the comedian, the center of attention, the rebel. Usually Damon loved Jeremy's rebellious spirit, but tonight I saw Damon's dark eyes burning laser beams at Jeremy, and I knew Jeremy could feel the weight of his best friend's stare.

"You can't bring that in there, either," the guard said, nodding down at the vodka bottle on the seat beside him.

"Yes, sir," Jeremy answered. "I won't."

We waited for what seemed like several minutes as the guard studied us through the driver's window. I was sure the guard was going to tell us to turn the van around and leave because we weren't taking this seriously, because we weren't ready to be vampires. But finally he spoke: "Keep your masks on the whole time you're in the house."

The guard backed away from Mel's window and nodded at the guard by the gate who was already punching a code into a little metal box on a pole. The metal gates with sculpted birds and designs on them swung open silently.

Mel drove forward, her pale hands gripping her steering wheel so tightly. She drove down the wide, curving driveway towards the house in the distance.

We found a parking space between a Maserati and a Mercedes, Mel carefully pulling her van in between the two vehicles.

"Damn, bro," Damon said, shoving Jeremy. Even though Damon tried to make it sound like a good-natured jab, I could hear the anger in his voice.

Jeremy didn't say anything. He seemed to have sobered up quickly. Maybe he'd been going along with all of this like everything was a joke, just something to do because he was bored, but I don't think whoever was running this game would go through the extravagance of this party if this game was just a prank.

"This is serious," Damon said, directing his words at all of us now. "The vampires take this very seriously." He stared at the massive house by the water, the bay stretching off into darkness with lights lining the distant shore. "This is bigger than us," he whispered to himself.

And I must admit that this was the moment I knew this wasn't just a game anymore. I felt nervous and I was practically shivering even though it was a warm night in late September. This was the first moment that I was worried that we were entering into something deeper than we had imagined, something far more dangerous than we had ever dreamed of. I had a panicky feeling at that moment; I didn't want to go into that house. I didn't want to commit to this anymore. I wanted to wait in the van, or maybe even run back to the three guards and beg them to let me back out, tell them that I had made a terrible mistake.

But I couldn't do that to Damon. He wanted this so badly, and I was going to suck up my fear and do this for him.

The party was amazing, no expense spared. A blur of strobe lights bounced around inside. Music played, thrumming through our bones, but not music that we were used to—something foreign-sounding, a woman singing in another language, her voice sexy and throaty, full of heartbreaking loss, but also arousing in a way that I couldn't understand. Beautiful naked men and women danced in tall metal cages suspended from the ceiling by chains; they writhed to the music like they were in a trance.

It looked like there were at least a hundred people gathered in a massive room just beyond the grand foyer. The party was a goth's dream party, an explosion of fetishes: beautiful women dressed in the skimpiest of dresses, skintight leather, shiny black vinyl, stiletto boots, metal buckles, silver jewelry and piercings, pale and creamy skin, dark skin, revealing clothing that showed off men's muscular arms and women's curvy legs, wet and full lips underneath Mardi Gras masks, watchful eyes—like animal eyes, like predatory eyes behind those masks. Some of the people danced together, entwined with each other, grabbing at each other violently, spinning their partners, bending them down and exposing their long and slender necks. Others gathered in small groups, many of them holding drinks in thick wine goblets. Everyone seemed to be drinking the same dark red wine.

All of the lights were turned down low and the strobe lights pulsed to the sensual music. A long mahogany bar took up nearly one wall where two masked bartenders served up the only drink offered. A few other partiers were out by the pool beyond the wall of sliding glass doors that had been opened up to allow the humid night breeze to blow in from the bay.

We were served the dark red wine. Jeremy gulped his down like he would any alcoholic drink. He was about to thrust his goblet at the bartender for refill, but he paused for just a moment like he was suddenly worried that he was going to collapse. I saw the confusion behind the eyeholes of his mask. He was unsteady on his feet, waiting for a wave of dizziness to pass.

Jeremy was drinking on the way here, I told myself. He's just had too much to drink already, that's all.

I glanced at the bartender who had a knowing smile carved into his pale face just underneath his mask.

Damon sipped his glass of wine, as did I. We were instructed to finish our glasses of wine by the bartender. But even if he hadn't told us that, I would have already known it, like it was some kind of unwritten rule. The wine was thick and tasted somewhat strange, sweet and salty at the same time, and there was a slight metallic aftertaste that I couldn't place. I could taste the wine in the drink, but this was unlike any wine I'd ever drunk. I had a suspicion of what was mixed with the wine right then and there, but I sipped it anyway.

And after a few sips I knew what Jeremy had experienced, an overwhelming rush of sensation that threatened to kick my legs out from under me. I wasn't much of a drinker, like I'd said before, so I didn't have any kind of experience with it like Jeremy and Ronnie did, but this was like nothing I'd ever felt before. I felt like I was floating, but it was more than that. There was a feeling of bliss, and of strength and power and energy. It felt like I'd been hungry and thirsty my whole life, and this was the first time that I'd ever truly been sated and nourished.

Damon would tell us later that he believed the wine had been spiked with blood—perhaps the virus-tainted ancient blood of vampires. I didn't want to believe that was true, but I had had the same suspicions as I drank the wine that night at the party. I thought a panicky feeling would rise up inside of me at the thought of that, but the wine had taken me to a place where fear couldn't touch me. I convinced myself later that the wine had been spiked with some kind of drug—not ancient blood—perhaps some kind of hallucinogen.

The rest of the night was a blur. We danced with each other as we sipped our wine. We talked with some of the others there, cordial conversations and exchanged pleasantries that I couldn't remember later. I wasn't slurring my words at the time, but I felt drunk with pleasure and bliss, drowning in it, letting it carry me away.

SEVENTEEN

THERON

"You don't remember anything else about the party?" Theron asked.

"No," Cyn said, shaking her head. "I remember talking to a woman who had some kind of Eastern European accent. I could tell she was beautiful even with her mask on, maybe the most beautiful woman I'd ever seen."

"But everything else was hazy."

"Yeah. Everything was kind of like a blur, but I still remember bits and pieces. You know how you wake up from a dream, but you can't remember all of it, only fragments, no matter how hard you try to remember?"

Theron nodded.

"It was like that. I know it was the wine we drank. But part of it was the awe of being in the mansion, being surrounded by that much wealth and beauty and power. The music was like nothing I'd ever heard before, a seductive calling that pulled at me. I talked to an older man with silver hair who was still muscled like a twenty-five year old athlete. I felt the power oozing from him, and from the others. I felt their confidence. I felt like I was being drawn to them, like I wanted to be a part of their secret club. I think I understood Damon's lust for it then. Jeremy swore he saw two famous athletes there among the crowd, a football player and a baseball player. Mel swore she saw a singer. Damon was sure many movers and shakers were there among the partygoers."

"Did you recognize anyone famous?" Theron asked.

"No. But I believed Damon and Mel."

Theron sat quietly in his office chair for a moment, saying nothing—he knew she had more to say. Her expression changed slightly, a darkness clouding it.

"Even though I felt bliss at that party, there was still a dread somewhere deep inside of me. There was this fear that I can't even describe. I felt like I had lost a part of myself inside that mansion, like a part of me had been stolen by them. I felt like panicking. But it also felt like I'd been drugged, like the core part of me wanted to do one thing, but something wasn't allowing me to do it. Kind of like wanting to move a part of your body, but you can't do it."

"When did you feel like yourself again?"

"About halfway home. The others were still stoked, still high on whatever drug they had sipped in the wine throughout the night—because I had convinced myself at that time that it had been a drug in that wine and not blood."

"But you don't think that now?"

"No. Now I'm sure it was blood."

Again, Theron didn't say anything. He wasn't going to challenge her belief in vampires and secret societies right now—he would at least listen to the rest of her story first.

Cyn continued her story. "Jeremy and Ronnie started sipping the vodka again as soon as we left the neighborhood, further dulling their senses into oblivion. I was getting worried that I was still going to be drunk when I got home, but like I said, the feeling wore off about halfway home. I felt like I was crashing hard, but I didn't want to show it. I tried to stay euphoric about the evening, but that panicky weight was pressing down on my chest again, making it hard for me to breathe."

"Did your parents know you were drinking?"

"No. I was totally sober by then. But they were pissed that I had stayed out so late again. I got my lecture. I got grounded. But we all knew I wasn't going to obey them. I had new masters to obey now."

"So you had a new task to complete after your reward?"

"Yes."

Theron watched Cyn for a moment. "But you were having reservations about completing the next task."

She nodded. "After the party that night, I felt this emptiness inside of me. Like I had been shown a glimpse into what the world was really like, what reality really was and not the pretend play that we all go along with, not the façade we try to trick ourselves into believing. I felt like all of life's dreams had been dashed in one night. But the others didn't see it that way. They were still high on the possibilities of becoming vampires. I tried to talk to Damon about my feelings, but he rationalized things for me, twisted what I was trying to say around to his view. And I let him. I still felt somewhat safe with Damon, and I had even tried to convince myself that I was wrong about the party."

"So you didn't want to do the next task. You didn't want to go on with the game?"

"I didn't want to, and for the first time I was really afraid."

Cyn was quiet for a moment, and that look was back on her face, the same look she'd had when she had admitted to stealing the woman's purse, confessing how she had hurt someone so badly, someone she didn't even know. Theron had seen that same look on people's faces many times before, not just embarrassment at having done something wrong or from being caught, but shame. When he'd been a cop, Theron always knew he had a suspect close to confessing when he saw that look on their face; he just needed to be patient and wait for the confession. And that's what he was doing with Cyn, just being patient and letting her tell her story in her own way. Eventually there would be some kind of confession—he knew it was coming.

"The next task came a few days after the party," Cyn said.

"So around the beginning of October," Theron said, jotting down a few more notes, trying to keep the timeline straight. It was almost Halloween now, so Cyn had to be getting close to the end of her story, to where it had led to tonight, leading to her confession—whatever that would be.

She nodded in agreement. "Yes. It seems so long ago now even though it's only been a few weeks. That's when it got so . . . so out of control."

"Out of control how?"

Cyn stared at Theron across his desk. "Like I told you, I was already scared. The party was supposed to be some kind of reward for us, but it had frightened me more than anything had so far. The party convinced me that this game was real. Those vampires were real. Or at least they *believed* they were real."

A cult. That's what Theron was thinking. Some kind of vampire cult that had Cyn convinced they were real.

"I already knew I didn't want to do the next task. Even before the text came, even before I knew what it was they wanted us to do, I already knew I couldn't do it."

"Did you tell Damon this? Or Mel?"

"No. I suffered in silence. I tried to convince myself that I needed to keep going. But when the text came, and when I entered my code and saw what we had to do, I didn't want to do it. The next task was actually two tasks in one, and I wasn't prepared to do either one of them. I called Damon up—I knew he and the others had already gotten their texts and punched their codes in. I knew they had already seen what we were supposed to do."

"What did you say to Damon?"

EIGHTEEN

CYN

I told Damon that I couldn't do the task.

"Yes, you can," he told me in a gentle voice. "You can do anything you want to."

"No, not this."

We were supposed to desecrate a church and renounce God. The masquerade party had been fun and seductive in its strange way, but I had also done a few things that I was ashamed of. I had committed crimes, and I knew the tasks were only going to get worse.

"You're not even religious," Damon said, actually chuckling a little like our task was no big deal. He seemed to be wondering why I was suddenly being so melodramatic.

"That doesn't have anything to do with it—I'm not doing this task."

Damon was silent as he stared at me for a moment. I was quiet, too. I hoped my silence was evidence of my resolution not to do this task. I hoped my silence was showing my strength, showing that I wasn't going to back down.

"Do you want this or not?" Damon snapped at me. The amusement was gone from his voice—he'd grown cold. I could tell an ultimatum wasn't far off now. I was scared of doing this task, but at that time I still might have been more afraid of losing Damon. I had no doubt right then that Damon would carry on without me if I chose to drop out of the game. He would walk away without even a look back at me.

"Yes," I finally answered. "I want this." I didn't want to do this task; I just wanted to be with Damon.

"If you want this, then you need to do this task with me."

Before I knew what I was doing, I was nodding.

He smiled. "So, you're going to do it?"

"Yes," I said, the word coming out in a rush of breath.

He grabbed me and kissed me. He held me.

I had always wondered how girlfriends could join their boyfriends on a crime spree. I had always wondered how those girls couldn't see when a line was being crossed. And I think I understood at that moment how a person could go so willingly even though they knew in their bones what they were doing was wrong and dangerous and hurtful to others. I wondered at that moment as I held Damon if I was already a vampire, if I had been somehow hypnotized. Before I even knew what I was doing, before I had even thought about it much more, I was agreeing to go with Damon and the rest of them that night.

Damon already had the perfect church in mind.

The small church was in a rural area. It didn't really look like the prototypical church: a white chapel with a steeple on top. This was just a large stucco building that looked like a big house with a lot of windows. There was a gravel parking area at one end of the building where the main doors were. The gravel area was pretty small so the rest of the churchgoers' cars and trucks must have parked on the Bahia grass, leaving dead spots and tire marks in the dry grass. A big sign at the corner of the property where two roads intersected advertised the church's service hours and the pastor's name.

I didn't want to know his name.

It was definitely not a wealthy church. The small-town congregation was probably made up of mostly elderly people. Judging from the size of the building, the place couldn't hold more than fifty people at a time. There were no security cameras and no signs warning of a security system.

There were some other houses in the area, but the closest one was at least a quarter of a mile away. Beyond the church, which sat on at least two acres of land, was a pine forest and a sea of palmetto shrubs. We parked in front of the section of woods that met the road and walked to the church from there in the midnight darkness. I had told Mom that I was sleeping at Mel's and Mel had told her parents that she was staying the night at my house. I knew Mel's parents wouldn't ever check on her, but I wasn't so sure about my mom and dad.

When we got to the church, Jeremy pried one of the windows open with an expertise I didn't know he had. It made me wonder if Damon and Jeremy did more than just deal drugs. He crawled in through the window, shining a small flashlight around but keeping his hand cupped in front of it to cut down on the light. He was inside maybe five minutes before coming back to the window, materializing from the darkness, a triumphant smile on his pale face, his eyes shining in the darkness. "Coast is clear," he whispered.

While we were waiting for Jeremy to come back to the window, I looked at Damon and then at Ronnie and Mel. Ronnie seemed to be the only other one of us who might've been having reservations about completing this task. It was a Saturday night so he didn't have to work the next day—Damon wasn't going to let Ronnie use his job as an excuse not to be here. Damon wasn't going to let any of us miss this opportunity.

One by one we crawled in through the window. Damon went in last and grabbed his backpack from the ground which held our tools of destruction.

The church was plain and modern. I guess I'd been imagining some kind of Catholic cathedral that we were going to vandalize, churches I saw in the movies with ceilings ten or twelve stories high above the congregation, stained glass windows, pews for thousands of worshippers, bleachers for a choir, a huge organ with flues climbing a wall, gold and marble everywhere. But a church was a church, that's what Damon had said on the way there—the instructions just said that it had to be a Christian church.

I walked from the main doors to the last row of pews, which were just wooden benches with cloth seats. The backs of the pews had racks for the hymn books and Bibles. Windows ran down both sides of the church walls, all of the windows had cheap plastic blinds covering them and parted curtains. Berber carpeting covered the floor and ran up the three steps onto a stage that took up the other end of the room. There was a pulpit in the middle of that stage and a piano off to the side. There were two big speakers at the front of the stage and track lighting hung from the ceiling. Mounted to the wall behind the pulpit was a gigantic wooden cross. There were some fake plants around the room, a few paintings hung on the walls back by the entrance doors and in the lobby where there was extra seating. The walls were painted a soft beige color, everything else trimmed in white.

Damon set his backpack down and pulled out some candles. He collected the candles in the middle of the floor between the last pews and the doors that led out to the front lobby. We gathered around the candles in a circle as Damon lit them, all of us sitting down on the floor.

I was still nervous about all of this. Not so much about getting caught anymore—I actually thought it would be a relief if the cops came busting in through the doors. I was nervous about what I had agreed to do: desecrating this church and renouncing God. Like Damon said, I wasn't religious, but that didn't mean that I wasn't a believer, or at least unsure about what to believe in. I found it kind of hypocritical that someone like Damon could believe so easily in something like vampires, but then be so sure that God didn't exist. But I think on the way to the church that night, I had changed my mind about Damon. I was sure then that Damon was a believer in God; he was just willing to turn his back on God to become a vampire.

As I sat there on the floor around the candles, I told myself that when I renounced God I would just pretend to do it. In my mind, I wouldn't really be doing it even as I spoke the words. God would understand, wouldn't He? He would forgive, wouldn't He?

NINETEEN

THERON

"Do you think God forgave you?" Theron asked.

Cyn was quiet for a moment before answering. Finally she shook her head. "I don't know. I hope so."

Theron remembered hearing about a church on Fulsome Road getting vandalized a few weeks ago. He was sure it was the same church that Cyn was talking about.

But it was more than just vandalism—he realized that now. They had been desecrating the church, renouncing their faith and renouncing God. He hadn't heard any more about the church, not really remembering if the police had caught the vandals, and now he realized that they hadn't. Theron was sure insurance would cover the church . . . maybe, or maybe the insurance company would find some way to weasel out of it.

"After we destroyed the inside of the church, the congregation helped fix it up again," Cyn said. The thought of it seemed to make her feel better. "I think they had some kind of neighborhood fundraising drive or something."

"Did you keep track of what happened with the church after that night?" Theron asked.

Cyn didn't answer at first. She just shrugged. "It was just a building," she finally said. "Buildings can be fixed. Sins can be forgiven."

"How exactly did you renounce God?" Theron asked.

"We did that before we started the desecration. Damon wanted to get it out of the way before we all went our separate ways, going wild in the church. Also, I think he was paranoid that we wouldn't complete that part of the task so he wanted to do it first. Like I said, we sat around the candles in a circle. We held hands. Damon seemed to have some kind of speech memorized. I don't know if it was something he had made up or something he'd found on the internet. Or maybe it was something they sent him in a text to say."

"What did he say?"

"I can't remember it word-for-word. And I wouldn't want to repeat it even if I could remember all of it. But it was basically us turning our backs on God and everything holy."

"That sounds more like Satanism than vampirism," Theron said.

"Damon told us it was all part of the conditioning, part of the preparation for us to leave our old lives behind. Once we were transformed, there could be no going back to our old lives. There could be no going back to our faith, our family, our rules and laws, our beliefs and values."

Theron felt like pressing Cyn about what exactly Damon had said in that church, the exact words, but he let it go.

"I felt ugly after saying those things, repeating the things Damon said. I felt evil. I felt irredeemable. Lost. And when we started trashing the place, I just went wild with the rest of them. I beat holes into the walls with a hammer while Jeremy spray painted obnoxious things on the walls. Damon said we would have to take something of value from the church so it would look like petty criminals had done this. Ronnie found a lockbox of money in an office and stuffed the whole thing down into the backpack. Mel kicked at the walls and tore pictures down, turned over the pews."

"What did Damon do?"

Cyn hesitated for a moment. "He said he wanted the cross for himself. He tore it down off of the wall. He . . . he turned it upside down, and he . . ." She didn't continue.

Theron wondered if Damon had urinated on the cross. But, from what he remembered, there was no physical evidence left behind at the crime scene. He would have to check on it later, call his friend Harris at the police station. Of course Theron knew that a vandalized church wasn't always the highest priority on the list when it came to crimes.

"I cried that night in bed," Cyn said. "I begged God for forgiveness. It was the first time I hated Damon, the first time I didn't feel like I was in love with him anymore. I think it was the first time I realized he wasn't really in love with me, either. He'd just been playing me, bringing me along on this stupid game with him. But I knew then that he loved that game and he loved the idea of being a vampire more than he loved me. Like I said before, if I dropped out of the game, I was sure he would be more than willing to leave me behind."

"Was that when you started being afraid of Damon?"

After another long pause from Cyn, she nodded. "Yeah. I think I was afraid of him a little by then. You should've seen him in that church. I knew Damon was wild, perhaps even potentially dangerous. I knew he had a dark side—it was one of the things that had attracted me to him—but this was too dark for me now, too dangerous. This fantasy world was becoming too real. Damon's belief in it was consuming him."

She paused for a moment and then went on. "I tried to talk to Damon. I tried to tell him how I felt. I hinted that I wanted out of the game."

"What did he say about that?"

"First, he treated me like a child—like he usually did. Then he tried again to sell me on the beauty, power, and freedom of being a vampire. But when he saw that those tactics weren't working anymore, he got angry. I was afraid he was going to attack me. He warned me about dropping out of the game. He warned me that I had agreed to go all the way with this. He warned me that they would come after me."

"The vampires?"

"Yes."

"And you think they are after you now?"

"Yes," she said, practically shouting the word out. "You saw one of them outside the Dairy Queen tonight."

"I saw *someone* standing there."

She stared at Theron, scowling at him like she suddenly distrusted him, like sitting here and opening up about all these secrets was suddenly the wrong thing to do. "You saw that man disappear tonight. I know you did."

Theron didn't know what he'd seen tonight—but it had been strange, he could admit that much to himself. And Cyn, she was obviously convinced all of this vampire stuff was true.

"I think they started watching me after that night at the church," Cyn said. "I don't know if Damon warned them somehow that I was thinking about quitting or if . . . if they just *knew* somehow. But I started seeing them out of the corner of my eye at night, hiding in the shadows, emerging from the darkness and then slipping back into it."

"Did you ever see any of their faces? Anyone you could identify?"

"No, but I could feel them. They didn't get close to me just then, but they were giving me a warning."

"You think those . . . those shadowy people that you saw after that night at the church could've been Damon or Jeremy? Maybe pretending to be vampires to either scare you or convince you that they were real."

"Maybe. I guess so. But I don't think so. The people I saw didn't feel like Damon or Jeremy. No, these people felt different."

"When did you drop out of the game? Did you complete the next task?"

"No. When I got the next text, when I punched in my code and saw what we had to do, I knew then that I wasn't going to continue with this game any longer."

#

CYN

The next task was to sacrifice an animal and drink its blood.

I couldn't do it. I told Damon that I couldn't do it. I had been willing to do some things that I hadn't been comfortable with, but this was way past the line for me.

We had gathered together at Ronnie's apartment since his uncle was gone again for the afternoon—out drinking himself into a stupor. Damon laughed off my refusal at first, but when he saw I was serious about quitting the game, he got angry again. I was afraid he was going to force me to come along, but I think there might have been some kind of rule in the Vampire Game about willing participants.

Jeremy suggested killing a dog, and Mel suggested a cat. They both thought that those animals would be easy to find. But Damon felt the animal needed to be a goat for some reason, some kind of religious symbolism or crap like that. He seemed to be trying to dissect each task, outthink the masters of the game by interpreting possible hidden meanings.

"That's it for me," I told Damon while we were gathered at Ronnie's apartment. I wanted the other three to hear that I was opting out—I wanted witnesses. I also felt like Damon was less likely to be violent with the other three around.

Damon tried for a while to convince me to keep going, even resorting to begging, but I wasn't going to kill an animal, not only because I didn't want to kill an animal, but also because I knew what all of this was leading up to—sacrificing a human. And I guess, deep down inside, I had to believe that the others knew where this was heading, too.

"What's the big deal?" Damon asked me. "All we have to do is kill an animal. Humans have been killing animals for hundreds of thousands of years."

I wasn't going to fall for Damon's warped logic.

"You eat meat," Damon said like he was accusing me of the act. "Someone had to kill those cows and chickens that you ate."

"Yeah, but not *me*."

"But you still ate the meat."

"Well, I've just decided to go vegan."

Damon sighed, not finding what I just said very funny. "It's just an animal. That's all."

"Yeah, but it's more than just killing an animal. We have to drink its blood."

"Yeah," Damon said. "What do you think we'll be doing eventually? What do you think vampires *do?*"

I stared at Damon, at a loss for words for a moment. I saw then that they all knew very well what these tasks were leading up to, and they were looking forward to it. My stomach turned as I thought of killing someone, draining the blood, drinking it down.

"Damon," I whispered as I backed up a step from Ronnie's table, getting closer to the apartment door. "This is . . . you know this is just a game, right? This isn't real."

He had an expression on his face like I had just slapped him. He stared at me in shock like I had just told him the Earth was flat.

"It's called the Vampire *Game*. It's just a game. That's all. We're not going to really turn into vampires, even if we kill someone and drink their blood. We won't be vampires, we'll just be murderers."

"Why are you acting like this?" Mel asked me.

I looked at her—my lifelong friend. I saw the hatred in her eyes then; she wasn't even bothering to hide it anymore. I met each one of their eyes, and I saw that none of them were going to back me up, none of them were going to be reasonable about this, none of them were going to face reality.

I was frightened. My boyfriend, his friends, and my best friend were all turning into monsters. I was sure I would be attacked by them at any moment.

"I've gone along with this game as far as I can," I told Mel, focusing on her, trying to get through to her. "I destroyed my grandmother's ring for this. I stole a woman's purse and probably got her fired for this. I desecrated a church. I've committed crimes, and now I'm done."

Damon managed to look hurt, angry, and disgusted all at the same time. He stared at me like I was a traitor. But I could also see that Damon was giving up on me, and I saw in his eyes that our relationship was over. He was turning cold again, mean. "They're not going to let you out of the game now. You're in too far now. You know too much."

A chill ran through me, and I imagined again the four of them attacking me. I imagined them jumping a few tasks ahead and making me their first human kill, or tying me up and stashing me at the abandoned house until that task came. I think the only thing that saved me was that none of them were going to disobey the game. But when that task inevitably came up, they would come looking for me.

"Too bad," I managed to answer Damon, trying to be brave but maybe not pulling it off so well. "Are you going to be able to kill someone when it comes to that?"

Damon didn't answer, but I saw the answer in his eyes.

I looked at each of the others. I knew Jeremy and Mel were all the way in now; they would follow Damon to the end of this game. Ronnie might not go all the way—I saw some hesitancy in his eyes—but in the end, Ronnie was a follower, and he would follow the others like the puppy dog he was.

Mel had a smirk on her face. I'm sure she'd been betting that I wouldn't make it all the way through the game; I'm sure that she'd been certain I would eventually let Damon down by walking away. I'm sure her intention the whole time was to be there for Damon, proving her worth and her allegiance to the game, when I bailed on them.

Fine with me, I thought as I walked away. My relationship with Damon was over—Mel could have him now if she wanted him. My friendship with Mel was also over for that matter.

I left Ronnie's house with a panic rising inside of me. I kept looking over my shoulder as I hurried down the steps to the ground. It was almost dark and so much of the world was hidden in shadows, where monsters could hide.

I walked for a while. I called my dad to come pick me up when I was a few blocks away. He wasn't happy about coming to get me, and I almost hung up. I was afraid that Damon was going to come after me. I was sure that I would hear his motorcycle racing down the street towards me at any moment. I was scared and I started crying on the phone.

My dad changed when I cried; he melted, suddenly concerned. He told me he would be there as quickly as he could.

I waited at a corner three blocks away from Ronnie's apartment. There were other houses around. It wasn't the best neighborhood, but at least there were a few people hanging out on their porches. It looked like there was some kind of party at one of the houses; a few men were gathered on the porch watching me. They were creepy, but I found that I was more afraid of Damon than those creeps. And I was even more afraid of the vampires that might be hiding in the night.

I kept all of those people on the porches in sight until my dad got there. He pulled up and I got into the car. He drove and I started crying again when we were only a few blocks down the road. He didn't say much, he just put his hand on my shoulder and pulled over so we could talk. He wanted to know what was wrong. My father was different then, suddenly he was someone I could talk to. I wondered where my father and mother had been for the last two years, why they had changed so much. But then I realized I was the one who had changed. It was me who had been gone these last few years.

My dad and I talked for a few minutes while he had the car pulled over. The windows were up and the doors were locked; I felt a little safer inside the car, but not completely safe. I told my dad that Damon and I were over.

"Did he hurt you?" my dad asked.

I assured him that he hadn't.

Dad had to ask if Damon had forced himself on me sexually. His face was red with embarrassment, but some of the redness was also from a building rage. I had never imagined my father as a violent man, but I saw in that moment that my dad could explode—I could see him punching Damon out.

I assured my dad that nothing like that had happened. I told him that Damon and I had ended our relationship, and I was just sad.

When we got back home, I talked more about it with my mom and dad. We sat in the living room. My sisters were in their bedrooms, but I'm sure they were doing their best to eavesdrop. I didn't tell my parents anything about the Vampire Game, not then, but I promised them that I was never going to be with Damon again. And they seemed happy about that.

Mom was scared I might be pregnant. I swore to her that I wasn't, and I thanked God for that. I assured them again that Damon hadn't hurt me and that he had never laid a hand on me in anger. But they seemed to need a reason for our breakup, so I told them some stuff about Damon never going anywhere in life, that he was never going to grow up, and I couldn't see myself with him in a long-term relationship and I knew there was no future for us. I was actually parroting back a lot of their lectures and warnings about Damon, and I don't think they even realized it; I saw the pride on their faces as they realized their little girl was finally growing up, realizing that their message had finally gotten through to me.

After our conversation, I told them that I had a headache and that I just wanted to take a hot bath and go to bed. I cried in the bathtub, and then in bed. I didn't want it to be over with Damon, I still felt like I loved him a little, but I didn't see how our relationship could continue any longer. I prayed that Damon would see things differently after our argument. I prayed that my walking out on him and the game would finally wake him up. I figured I would give him a day or two to think about things, and I convinced myself that he would call me by the next evening.

TWENTY-ONE

THERON

"Did he call you the next day?" Theron asked Cyn.

"No. The next night they stole a goat from someone's farm—someone that Jeremy knew, a friend of a friend or something. They took the goat to a field to sacrifice it. They said some kind of prayers or something. Again, I don't know if the prayers were something the website had instructed Damon to say or if it was something he had made up on his own."

"How do you know all of those details?"

"Mel told me everything about the sacrifice the day after they did it. I called her up, hoping to pump some information out of her, but secretly hoping that they hadn't gone through with the task. She was a little guarded about Damon, but she was happy to tell me everything they had done."

"You didn't see her at school?"

"No. I hardly ever saw her at school anymore—she was skipping most days. I told her that it was going to eventually catch up with her and she was going to fail school, but I guess when you're going to become a vampire, what does school matter anymore?"

"Did she say anything else about the sacrifice?"

"She said they cut the goat's throat and drained the blood into a big metal bowl. They poured the blood from the bowl into a bottle so they could each drink from it. I don't know if they each took a sip or they drank all of it. She didn't tell me and I didn't want to know. She said they left the body of the goat in the field."

"Did she say which field?"

"Yeah. Not too far away from the abandoned house on Allen Road."

Theron wrote that down on his notepad.

"But they took the goat's head and left it at the church we had desecrated. I guess they drove by in Mel's van and Jeremy threw the goat's head out through the side door. She said it hit the front doors and then bounced off of them, landing right there in the walkway.

"I asked Mel about Damon, but like I said, she didn't say much, being purposely vague. And I swear I could hear her smiling when she talked about him, like she was hiding a secret. She seemed to be gloating now that I had been kicked out of their club. I hadn't realized how much she must have secretly hated me all these years, how she had sat on that hatred and let it fester."

"Did Damon ever ask you to get back together with him?"

Cyn looked down at her hands for a moment. She was fidgety again, like she needed another cigarette soon. "No."

"What about the game? Did he try to get you back in?"

"He called me a few nights later. He told me that the vampires were angry that I'd left the game."

"He had contact with them?"

"He didn't say how he knew they were angry, just that they were. He said that they really didn't want Mel, Jeremy, or Ronnie—the whole point was to get the two of us. We were the special ones, and they were just willing to take our friends into the game to get the two of us. He said they'd been watching the two of us for months before they sent the invitation to us."

"So he asked you to rejoin the game?"

"No, not right then. He told me again that it was too late for me to rejoin the game. I hadn't completed my task and entered my code. I don't really know why he was calling me if I couldn't rejoin the game. It almost seemed like he was trying to warn me."

"So you didn't have any contact with any of them after that phone call with Damon?"

"It was over between me and them. Like I said, I didn't see Mel in school anymore. I called and texted her a few times, but she never got back to me." Cyn paused for a moment. "Then I heard about things happening, and I was sure it was them. I heard about a house burning down a few weeks ago."

Theron had heard about that, too.

"The house that burned down was empty so no one was hurt or killed," Cyn said. "I watched the news. They were calling the fire arson. They didn't have any suspects, but I knew it was them."

"Why didn't you call the police then?"

"Because I didn't really have any proof. What was I supposed to say? That my friends were trying to become vampires and they were completing tasks they found on an internet website, and I think they're responsible for the crimes being committed these days?"

Theron didn't respond.

Cyn exhaled a frustrated sigh. "Every terrible thing I heard about on the news I suspected was them. A week later someone was throwing rocks from an interstate bridge. I don't know if it was them, but I couldn't help thinking that it was."

"What about the Vampire Game? Did you try to log back in?"

"Yeah, but my code wouldn't work anymore. I was locked out."

"Do you remember your code?" Theron pushed his notepad across the desk to her. "Could you write it down?"

She wrote the code down and slid it back to him. "It won't work. The website is still there on the dark web, but you can't do anything with it unless you have the code. And this was the last code I used. They change codes with each task."

Theron thought he could still find someone to track the source of the website, but everything was probably mired in layers and layers of protection: email addresses that bounced around the world, servers in Russia and Eastern European countries, accounts linked to dead people.

"Even though I wasn't talking to Damon anymore, I felt like I was being watched," Cyn said. "I felt like I was being followed. When I was at school waiting for my mom to pick me up, I saw a man at the edge of the school property, way out by the fence. He was tall and thin, wearing all black. A black trench coat. Sunglasses."

"Did you report the man to the school? Tell anyone else about him?"

"No. I didn't think anyone would believe me. Besides, when I looked back again, the man was gone. It was like he was there for a minute, and then the next minute he was gone."

Like the man we saw tonight, Theron thought.

Cyn nodded like she was reading Theron's mind. "I think that man in the Dairy Queen parking lot was the same guy I saw at my school. I'm sure of it."

"And you think that man tonight, and the one you saw at your school, are vampires?"

Cyn didn't say anything—she just nodded.

"I thought vampires couldn't come out during the day."

"Damon told me that was a myth. He explained it this way: vampires can go out into the daylight, but they don't like the sun very much. He said the sun saps their strength, speed, and energy."

"But the sunlight doesn't kill them."

"Damon said it didn't. He said a lot of the myths about vampires were things made up by horror writers and Hollywood producers. He told me garlic had no effect on vampires at all, and vampires could see their reflections in mirrors. He said crucifixes had no power over vampires, but they didn't like them because of their hatred for God and anything holy. Vampires couldn't fly. They couldn't turn into bats or other animals. They couldn't turn into smoke."

"But they live forever."

"Their aging has just slowed way down, like ten years to them is like a hundred years to us. Something about the process does something fundamental to their bodies at a cellular level, changing their hormones, cell structures, DNA, and other physical things. Somehow it makes their immune system super strong, their pain sensations dulled, their muscles stronger and quicker, their eyesight and hearing superhuman. But their power doesn't just come from their speed and strength—their power is also the cabal, the power of their numbers and devotion to each other. They are in positions of power all over the world, and they protect each other. They're like a Mafia family, but a Mafia family on steroids."

"So vampires are not really the undead?"

"No. They're still alive. You don't have to die to become a vampire. You just need to be infected by the virus."

"Did they come for you?" Theron asked Cyn. "Did Damon try to kill you?"

Cyn didn't answer the question for a moment, and then she spoke: "Damon called me one more time."

"What did he say?"

TWENTY-TWO

CYN

Damon called me up and tried to warn me not to quit the game. He changed his story suddenly, telling me that I could rejoin the game if I wanted to.

"I talked to some of them online," Damon told me on the phone. "On a secret message board."

I knew Damon was lying. I knew the rules of the game were set in stone. I knew he was trying to coax me out of my house, trying to get me to meet him at some location so I could become their first kill.

"Meet me," Damon whispered into the phone. "I want you back. I love you. I don't care if you're not a vampire. We can still be with each other. I know we can find a way."

Another lie. All lies. I could hear the desperation in his voice. Was he frightened in some way? Was I some kind of loose end that needed to be tied up pretty soon?

"I can't do this," I told him. "I don't want to talk to you anymore." I was close to crying, but I didn't want Damon to hear me cry. I didn't want to give him that victory, so I tried to be angry even though I was literally shaking. I wanted to sound cold and indifferent to his pleas.

Damon was silent for a moment. I could hear his breathing so I knew he was still there on the phone. I could tell he was nervous. I knew I was that loose end that he needed to take care of. Not only a loose end for him, but also for the cabal. I would need to be dealt with eventually. I wondered if Damon had been ordered to clean things up. I wondered if they were threatening to end the game for the four of them, ending their chances at becoming vampires if they didn't take care of me. Nothing would hurt Damon more, and I think he would've done anything to stay in the game. It was the first time I'd ever heard Damon so nervous. He wasn't just nervous about possibly getting killed by the vampires, but maybe even more nervous about disappointing them, of failing at his task and losing his chance at immortality, at his chance to belong to a community that he'd been born to be a part of. Everything was on the line for Damon.

"Come with me," Damon whispered in his most seductive voice. "Come with me to the house." He meant the abandoned house. I'm sure he had set some kind of trap there for me. Or maybe even a trap for me and Ronnie, or Mel. Or all of us. Maybe Damon was going to run away by himself to the cabal after the rest of us were dead. I could see it now, maybe Damon had been telling the truth about the vampires only wanting the two of us, and the other three were just dead weight that would have to be sacrificed eventually—just three more missing teenagers, runaways, just three more to add to the statistics. Well, four more if you counted me.

"I can't go anywhere with you," I told him.

"Then I'll come to you," Damon said. His voice had turned so cold again, so evil. He hung up.

I tried to call him back, but all I got was his voicemail. I knew then that Damon was coming that night, and I had no choice but to tell my parents everything.

Of course my mom and dad thought I was overreacting. They knew I was scared—there was no faking how frightened I was—but they figured that I had fallen for Damon's scary stories, believing the wild things he had told me over the last year we'd been together.

"Nothing's going to happen," my father said. "People like Damon are nothing but a bunch of talk."

I knew my dad didn't have a gun in the house, but I could tell that he secretly hoped Damon might come sneaking around so he could confront my ex-boyfriend, perhaps knock him out or even beat him senseless. My dad wasn't an imposing man at all; he was a middle-aged man with a potbelly who worked in an office all day, but there was something in his eyes that night, some storm of violence that he controlled most of the time. I guess a threat to a father's daughter could turn any man into a savage fighter.

But my father was seriously underestimating Damon—he didn't know how dangerous Damon was. He didn't know how fully absorbed Damon was into this world of vampires, this fantasy of his. I was sure that Damon was mentally ill at that point, and I felt like I wasn't getting that concept across to my dad.

I begged my dad to call the police, but he told me that there was no real proof that a threat had been made, nothing recorded that he could show the police.

"He threatened me," I told my father. "Isn't that enough?"

My dad kissed me on the forehead and gave me a hug. "I promise I won't let anything happen to you."

But I wasn't so sure my dad could handle this.

Later that night I lay in my bed wide awake. I had checked all of the doors and windows twice before going to bed. I told my two sisters about Damon threatening me and the possibility of him showing up that night. I was sure I had them sufficiently scared enough to call 911 if they saw Damon outside or heard him trying to break in.

I knew I wasn't going to school the next day so I resigned myself to staying awake through the night. I'd even made some coffee and poured it into a thermos. I kept the thermos on the table next to the bed. I kept my bedroom light off and the curtains open so I could see outside; the moon lit up the side yard.

I was worried about Damon, but I was even more scared that I might see the same vampire I'd seen at my school. But I rationalized with myself that the cabal would want to give Damon a chance to complete this task himself, to prove himself.

About two o'clock I jumped awake. I had drifted off to sleep. I sat up and stared at the window. There was a noise outside, some kind of scratching sound; it was a soft noise but I definitely heard it.

I got up and crept to my bedroom window. I crouched down low, peeking out at the side yard. The backyard and side yard were fenced in, and the wooden fence created a deep shadow. The middle of the yard was splashed with moonlight. But even in the shadow created by the fence, I saw someone standing there in the corner.

It was Damon.

He emerged from the shadows, stepping out into the yard, the moonlight exposing him. He wore black clothes, with his black trench coat over everything. He walked towards me, but it seemed more like he was gliding towards the window, his biker boots just inches above the grass, his movements barely perceptible. His pale face seemed to float in the darkness like an alabaster mask framed by his dark hair.

He was right outside my bedroom window seconds later, his hands grabbing at the stucco ledge at the bottom of the window, white fingers poking out of black fingerless gloves. The lower half of his face was smeared with blood; it looked like mud in the moonlight. His white teeth shined brilliantly among the stains that looked like a ghoulish beard and mustache. His eyes were wild, his smile maniacal. He stared at me, whispering words I couldn't hear through the glass, but he was still smiling the whole time.

I was panicking then, crawling backwards along the floor away from the window. I was afraid to look at him, but more afraid to look away. I was at my desk a few seconds later, grabbing my cell phone. I dialed 911 and heard a woman's voice squawking at me from the phone.

Damon was still at the window, still whispering, his fingers still caressing the ledge underneath the window, his eyes still wild, his smile still white against his bloodstained face.

"He's here!" I yelled into my phone at the 911 operator. I got to my feet and turned away from the window. "He's right outside my window!"

"Who's outside your window, ma'am?" the 911 operator asked.

I looked back at my window. Damon was gone.

TWENTY-THREE

THERON

"The police came?" Theron asked.

"Yes," Cyn answered. "My dad wasn't happy about me calling them. He told me I should've let him handle it, but I think my mom and sisters were relieved that I had called the police."

"What did the cops say when they got there?"

"They interviewed me, took my statement. There were two of them. They did a quick search around our house. They said they would follow up the next day with some questions for the neighbors. They also said they would question Damon and his mother some time tomorrow. But I knew that none of it was going to get anywhere. Damon's mother would stick up for him like she always did, and if they talked to Damon he would be as cool under pressure as he always was."

"Did you tell the police about the Vampire Game?"

"No. I wanted to, but I was afraid they would think I was nuts. I felt like they would take this more seriously if they thought Damon was just some psycho stalker ex-boyfriend. Maybe they would pick up on his peculiar interests just from the way he was dressed when they interviewed him, build up an instant prejudice and suspicion the way cops sometimes did. I was sure Mel, Jeremy, and Ronnie were at my house with Damon that night, but I hadn't seen those three, and I didn't want to complicate things by telling the police that they might have been there. I wanted them to go after Damon first."

"But nothing happened."

"No. I think the police were chalking my complaint up to a couple of teenagers going through a spat. I was sure Damon would lie convincingly if he was ever interviewed by the police. I was sure the police would give Damon a subtle warning to leave me alone and to move on to other fish in the sea."

"What did your parents say about this now?"

"My dad pretended to be a little angry after the police left our house that night. I don't think he wanted to admit it, and he never would've admitted it to me, but I think he was frightened at that moment. I don't think he really ever believed Damon would actually come to our house in the middle of the night. I think he was realizing at that moment how dangerous Damon had become. I hadn't told the police about the blood on Damon's face, but I had told my mom and dad about it. They agreed with me that it was a good idea to leave that little detail out when I talked to the police, along with the whole vampire thing."

"But they believed you about the blood on his face?"

Cyn shrugged. "I don't know. My mom thought it might have been mud on Damon's face, or even makeup. She also suggested that Damon might have used fake blood to freak me out. She even suggested that what I thought I'd seen might have been a shadow on his face, or even my imagination. My father agreed with her, even suggesting that I might have imagined the whole thing."

"Why would he think that?"

"For two reasons. One reason was because I admitted that I had just woken up when I saw Damon at my window. My mom and dad knew I was scared, and my dad proposed the idea that maybe I had been dreaming the whole thing and dialed 911 while I was still half asleep."

"What was the other reason?"

"There weren't any footprints outside my bedroom window. There was no sign of the blood I saw on Damon's face wiped on the gate, the fence, or the ledge below my window. There was no sign of forced entry to the gate, even though my dad had locked it from the inside."

"He could've climbed over the fence."

Cyn nodded. "Yeah, he could have. But part of that side yard is dirt where the grass has died. It had rained earlier that evening and the dirt had turned to mud. There should've been a footprint somewhere."

"What are you trying to say?" Theron asked. He wondered if Cyn was trying to suggest that Damon had floated across the side yard to her window. She had described him as gliding towards her window.

She shrugged. "I'm saying there were no footprints anywhere in the side yard. The police said the same thing."

"So your parents were sure that you had imagined the whole thing since there were no footprints?"

"Yeah. But I saw him. I know I did."

Theron nodded. "But it sounds like your parents doubted you."

"They doubted me, I'm sure of that. But I think they also believed me just a little. And my dad started taking it more seriously when Damon came back the next night."

TWENTY-FOUR

CYN

It was pretty late when Damon came back the next night. I had gone to bed, but after my parents and sisters were in bed, I went back out to the living room and waited on the couch near the window that looked out onto the street. I knew Damon would be back, and I had my phone ready—not just to call 911, but also to take a photo of him. I was angry at myself for not taking a photo of him the night before.

I sat there in the darkness for a while. I didn't want to turn on any lights or the TV; I wanted Damon to see a dark house and think we were all asleep.

Without really remembering it, I had drifted off to sleep. I snapped awake just like I had the night before. Some kind of noise had roused me from sleep, yet my conscious mind didn't know what it was. I sat up on the couch and looked at the front door. It was wide open.

Damon sat in the recliner on the other side of the living room—my dad's chair. Damon had turned the chair towards the wall so I could only see the back of the chair and his arm. He was silent as he sat there, just breathing quietly. His arm was sheathed in the trench coat sleeve, his pale hand in the black fingerless gloves.

I sat there frozen on the couch, sitting on the edge of it, ready to bolt, ready to run past him down the hall to my parents' bedroom, or maybe even out the open front door. I needed to do something. I could feel the energy building inside of me, erupting into a panic.

"Cyn," Damon whispered as his fingers clawed at the arm of the recliner. He turned around in the chair, and even though it was dark I could see him clearly. His face was so pale in the darkness, and that same dried blood was smeared on his face again, caked around his mouth . . . like he'd been feeding. His teeth were sharp and so brilliantly white compared to the dark blood that looked black in the moonlight that shined in through the open front door. His eyes were wild and insane, bulging from his face. He looked hungry and wild, and then he jumped out of the chair at me . . .

I woke up from the dream, sitting up on the couch, practically hyperventilating. My heart was thundering. I looked around the living room for Damon, but he wasn't there. I grabbed my cell phone and pushed the button to light it up. It was two o'clock in the morning. I jumped up from the couch and checked the front door—it was still locked.

I stood there for a moment, trying to get my breathing under control. I knew it had only been a nightmare, but I was also sure that something else had woken me up. It was like I knew Damon was near, like I could feel him now. I listened for the sound of Damon's motorcycle, thinking he might be riding up to our house at that moment. But then I thought Damon wouldn't use his bike—he would come with Mel in her van so all of them could come together.

I crept back to the couch and looked out the living room window right behind it, keeping low.

I saw Damon outside; he was standing on the sidewalk across the street. He stood like a shadow, just out of the glow of the streetlight, which shined down a yellowish-orange circle of light in the street and on the sidewalk. He was dressed just like he'd been the night before, all in black. His long hair hung down free to his shoulders, his face hidden in the darkness. The bottom of his trench coat flapped a little in the night breeze as he stood there.

My heart was thumping hard as I watched him, but Damon just stood there.

I had to get my dad. I backed off the couch, crouching down on the floor. I kept low as I raced across the living room and then to the hallway. I rushed into my parents' bedroom. Both of them were sleeping. I went to my dad's side of the bed and nudged him.

He snapped awake. "Whatisit?"

"It's him. Damon's outside."

It seemed to take my dad only a millisecond to comprehend what I had just said. He sat up like a rocket, swinging his feet over the side of the bed. He was dressed in a white T-shirt, a pair of boxers, and he had black socks on his feet. He fumbled at the nightstand for his glasses. I hurried back to the door while he grabbed his robe that he'd thrown over a wingback chair.

Mom turned over. "What's going on?" she whispered.

My dad didn't even answer her. He followed me to the living room.

"Keep the lights off," I told my dad.

We hurried through the darkness to the sofa and looked out the window. I expected Damon to be gone, and again I was cursing myself for not taking a photo with my phone when I had the chance.

But Damon was still out there, still standing in the same spot across the street.

"That's Damon?" my dad whispered. "You're sure of it?"

"Yes," I told him. And I *was* sure of it. I had my cell phone in my hand then and I bolted to the front door. I had more courage now that someone was awake with me out in the living room—especially my father.

"What are you doing?" There was alarm in his voice.

I didn't answer him. I opened the front door and rushed out onto the porch. I held my phone up and I took a picture, the flash going off. I took another one, keeping it aimed at the same place.

My dad was out on the front porch a few seconds later. "Where did he go?"

I lowered my phone and looked at the streetlight where Damon had been standing. He was gone.

My dad walked to the edge of the porch and then down the steps to the little cracked walkway that went across the front lawn to the driveway. He looked up and down the street, at the other homes that disappeared into the darkness. The night was quiet; there were no sounds of cars or even a barking dog. Nothing.

Mom was out on the porch a moment later, wrapped in her robe. "What's going on?" she asked, but I had a feeling she knew why we were out there.

"Damon was here," I told her.

She looked at Dad as he walked back up the steps.

"I saw him," Dad said, nodding his head and adjusting his glasses. "He was standing right over there by the streetlight." He hitched a thumb back in that direction.

"What was he doing?" Mom asked, drawing her robe tighter around her body.

"Just standing there," Dad said and then looked at me.

I nodded. "That's all I saw him doing."

"Should we call the police?" Mom asked.

Dad shrugged. "I don't think they're going to do anything about it. There's no law against someone standing on the sidewalk."

Mom seemed nervous. "Let's get back inside. We can talk about this in there."

We went back inside, and I knew that they believed me now about Damon. Maybe they didn't believe the whole vampire thing, but they knew then that Damon was far more dangerous than they had imagined.

TWENTY-FIVE

THERON

"Do you still have the photo on your phone?" Theron asked Cyn. She pulled the photo up on her phone and then slid the phone across the desk to Theron. He stared at the image for a few seconds. It wasn't a clear photo, just a shadowy and slightly blurry figure standing near the glow of a streetlamp.

"I know it's hard to see him," Cyn said defensively. "But you can see someone standing there."

Theron nodded and handed the phone back to Cyn. "Do you have any other photos of Damon and your other friends?"

"I'll send them to your phone. What's your cell number?"

Theron plucked a business card out of the plastic holder and handed it to her. His cell phone number was at the bottom.

Cyn went to work scrolling through her phone with the quick, practiced movements of a teenager. A minute later Theron heard the beep on his phone indicating that he had new text messages, but he didn't bother looking at them.

"If you want me to look into this for you, then you're going to need to give me all of their addresses, and any other information you can think of." He flipped a page in his notebook and slid it towards her with the pen.

Cyn scribbled down a few lines on the paper.

"So you never called the police that night after you saw Damon again?" Theron asked as Cyn jotted down the information he needed.

"No. I wanted to, but my mom and dad didn't. We talked to the police the next day when they came back for a follow-up."

"And your dad told them that he saw Damon standing outside?"

"Well, he wouldn't go that far. He told them that he saw *someone* standing out there."

"Did you show the police the photo on your phone?"

"Yeah. But as you can see, it's hard to make out any details. And they said the same thing my dad said, that it wasn't illegal for someone to stand on the sidewalk across the street from your house. They talked to Damon's mom again the next day, but she swore that Damon had been home all night. She even told the police that I had an overactive imagination and that I had accused Damon of doing things and that's why he broke our relationship off."

"What about that other person you saw at your school? And the one we saw at the Dairy Queen tonight. You don't think the man you saw outside your house could've been that person?"

"Maybe, but I'm positive it was Damon. I know Damon. I know his clothes, his hair, the way he stands. I know everything about him. And it was . . . I know it's going to sound stupid, but I could *feel* him out there."

"So you're sure it was Damon standing outside your house, and now you think he's going to attack you?"

"Yes."

Theron wanted to ask Cyn what he was supposed to do about all of this, but he didn't.

As if she'd read his mind, she answered him: "I just need some help. The police won't help. My parents aren't helping very much. I haven't been going to school." She stopped, like she was holding her breath, like she was doing her best not to cry. "I . . . I just don't know what else to do."

Theron still wasn't sure what she was asking of him, but he could tell that she was desperate for help. The least he could do was investigate this further, see what he could do to help. "I should go talk to Damon. And your friends."

Cyn nodded, but then she shook her head. "They haven't been around for the last few days."

"How do you know that?"

"My dad said the police were trying to get a hold of them. I heard from some other friends that they haven't been around."

"Where do you think they are?"

Cyn shrugged. "I don't know. I think they might be planning their first kill. Or they've already done their first kill and now they're laying low."

"What makes you think they've done their first kill?"

"I don't know. I heard about a missing girl down in Pasco or Polk County. Her name is Ashley Lowe. She's my age and pretty. I've been watching a lot of local news lately, searching articles on the internet. They're saying Ashley Lowe ran away from home, but it doesn't seem like her parents or friends think that's true."

Theron didn't say anything.

"That's who they would go after, teenagers, ones that could be easily written off as runaways. Or they might go after homeless people. There are people missing every day. More people are missing every day than are murdered. I saw that statistic somewhere when I was looking stuff up."

Theron knew there were a lot of people reported missing every year in America—the number was staggering—but the majority of those were runaways or parents abducting their own children after custody battles.

"I will look into this starting tomorrow," Theron told Cyn.

She breathed out a sigh of relief and smiled at him. "Thank you. Thank you for helping me."

"I'm not promising anything."

"If you could just get some kind of evidence so the police will believe me, maybe that would help. Or try to get them to back off."

Theron nodded. "I'll see what I can do." He stood up. "Let me give you a ride back home."

Cyn stood up. She looked at the glass door that led outside, and then she looked back at Theron. "I know you don't believe me about the vampires, but at least believe me that these people that Damon is involved with are dangerous. You need to be careful."

"I will," Theron promised her.

TWENTY-SIX

THERON

After a few fitful hours of sleep, Theron went to work on Cyn's case the next morning—his *only* case at the moment. He heated up a breakfast sandwich in the microwave oven and ate a few bites, washing it down with a can of Coke. He brushed his teeth in the small bathroom, got dressed, and slipped his shoulder holster on. He had a pair of handcuffs in a leather pouch on his belt. He put his suitcoat on, covering everything up.

There were a lot of things he wanted to do today, but the first thing he wanted to do was check out the abandoned house on Allen Road. Damon and his friends probably wouldn't be there, but it couldn't hurt to check out the house in the daylight. He at least wanted to get a layout of the place because he planned on going back there later tonight, possibly staking the place out if he had nothing better to do.

On the way out to the abandoned house, Theron called Harris—a friend of his from back when he'd been a cop.

"Hey, Theron," Harris said into the phone. "Haven't heard from you in a while. How have you been?"

"Hanging in there," Theron replied.

"Hey, I heard about your . . . your diagnosis. And I'm sorry, man."

"Nothing to be done about it," Theron told him. A year ago, after some chest pains, Theron had gone to see a doctor. After a myriad of tests were done, the doctors informed Theron that he had a heart defect—a genetic disorder that his doctor called the widow maker. For some reason, because of his genetics, plaque was building up in his arteries and in his heart at a faster rate than normal. His father had died in his mid-fifties, and his older brother had died two years ago from a massive heart attack. No males lived past the age of sixty on his father's side. The doctors put a stent in one of his arteries for now, but it was only a quick fix. When his heart attack came, it would be like a thunderclap; he would just collapse, probably be dead before he even hit the ground. The doctors told him that this disorder affected a lot of people, and most of them didn't even know they had the defect until it was too late.

Was that supposed to make him feel better, that there were others like him with ticking time bombs inside their chests? He wished he was ignorant of this news like some of the others were; he thought it might be better to just drop dead one day rather than waiting around and wondering every minute of the night when it was going to happen.

Of course the doctors recommended that he quit smoking and drinking, which he did right away. They also recommended changes in his diet and getting some regular exercise, lose a few pounds. He asked the doctors how much it would help. They just shrugged and gave some noncommittal answers; things like: doing something is better than doing nothing.

"I was wondering if I could ask a favor," Theron asked Harris.

"Anything," Harris said without hesitation. It seemed like he wanted to do anything to help a man with a death sentence.

"I was wondering if you could send some info my way."

"Sure. What do you need?"

"Could you send me any info you have on missing persons over the last two weeks?"

"Sure. What areas?"

"Uh, several counties: Hillsborough, Pinellas, Polk, Pasco, Sumter, Hernando, and Citrus."

"Okay. I can get that together and send it to you. Same email?"

"Yeah. That would be a big help."

"Looking for anything in particular?" Harris asked, fishing for something.

"Yeah, there is one thing. A missing teenager from either Polk or Pasco County. Her name is Ashley Lowe."

"Okay," Harris said like he already knew exactly who Theron was asking about. "Any particular reason?"

"It's for a case I'm working on."

After a little more small talk and some empty promises about getting together for a few beers, Theron hung up. He wanted to go by each of the kids' houses and see if they were home, or at least talk with their parents or whoever they were living with, but it was still too early to do that. He'd go to the abandoned house first.

TWENTY-SEVEN

THERON

Theron ended up driving past the abandoned house twice on Allen Road before finally seeing the driveway nestled among the overgrown brush and weeds. He turned his car around and drove back to the splash of dirt and sand just off of the lonely, two-lane road. He pulled off the road and saw the dirt trail a little better now.

He put his car in park and shut it off. He got out and stood next to his car, listening for any sounds. He looked up and down the road, but there wasn't much to see except woods. A little farther down he'd seen a few homes set far off from the road, but the nearest one had to be at least two miles away. Theron had seen large fields on his way out here, a few cattle ranches, acres of struggling orange groves, stands of woods and palmetto brush, but that was about it.

The abandoned house couldn't be seen from the road, but it had to be somewhere back there beyond the brush and trees. He walked down the winding trail in the brush. Thirty feet down the trail, he saw the metal gate. There was a chain wrapped around the end of the rusted gate and tethered to a wooden post, but there was no lock on it. He unwrapped the chain and pushed the gate open.

He walked through the gate and down the dirt trail, looking around at the sea of palmetto plants and brush. Pine and palm trees stood here and there, but when he rounded another bend in the trail, he saw a small forest of trees in the distance. And there, poking out of those trees, was the roof of a house.

Theron went back to his car and started it; he drove down the trail and through the gate. Once he was past the gate, he parked so he could get out and close the gate again, wrapping the chain around the end of the gate and the post. It was a pain in the ass, but if Damon and the others came by he didn't want them to know that someone had discovered the gate in the brush. He got back in his car and drove down the dirt trail, which was a little worn down by recent traffic.

There was a clearing near the dilapidated house, but no cars were parked there, and no motorcycle. There was another smaller clearing beyond a gigantic island of brush and palm plants to the right, and Theron backed his car up into this spot. If he pulled behind the wall of vegetation, he had a slight view of the parking area near the house but his car was still hidden. When he came back tonight, he would park in this spot.

He got out and touched the butt of his gun in the shoulder holster, an unconscious habit he had. He also made sure he had his cell phone with him in his pocket. He walked across the larger clearing towards the house. It was a one-story, block and stucco home with a shingled roof, the shingles black with mold and mildew. The home looked kind of small, no bigger than fifteen hundred square feet, Theron guessed. There was no garage attached to the house, but part of the roof covered a concrete parking area that could probably fit two cars side by side. The corner of the roof over the parking area was sagging, and it probably leaked when it rained. The shrubs and brush had grown up close to the house on all sides. Massive oak trees towered all around the home, a few of the branches practically touching the roof in some places.

Theron walked down the beaten-down path through the brush and weeds to the front door. The roof formed a little front porch area here, just big enough for a couple of rocking chairs. The front door was recessed back into the home and there was a larger window to the left of the front door, and a smaller window to the right—probably a bedroom window. He peeked in the smaller window, but he couldn't see anything but darkness.

On the other window—probably the living room window—there was a piece of paper taped to the glass. The paper had been yellowed by the sun and a corner of it had been torn away; the paper was barely hanging on. It was a condemnation notice from the county, and a warning to stay out of the house and off of the property. There was another similar notice taped to the front door.

Theron knocked on the front door. He waited a moment, listening.

No sounds from inside the house.

He knocked again. Louder this time—a police knock.

Still no answer, no hushed whispers, no sound of rushing feet.

He fished out a pair of latex gloves from an inside suitcoat pocket and slipped them on. He tried the doorknob. It was locked. The doorknob looked newer, but the door seemed flimsy, like if he pulled on it hard enough he could force it open—but he didn't want to do that. He dug a credit card out of his wallet, and after a few seconds of jiggling the edge of the card around the lock, the door sprang free. He stuffed the card back into his wallet.

"Hello?" he said as he opened the door slowly.

No answer.

He opened the door all the way. It was murky inside the house, but he saw that the door opened up to a living room area. There were a few pieces of furniture, but nothing much else.

"Hello?" he said as he entered the house. "I'm a private investigator. If anyone's here, I need you to identify yourself."

There wasn't anyone there; Theron was sure of it now.

His first impression of the house was that it was remarkably clean for being an abandoned house. The floor was clear of debris and swept. He had expected to be assaulted with mildew smells and musty odors, but the place smelled clean, like cleanser and air freshener had been used recently. There was also the scent of candles, a vanilla scent and the hint of oranges.

It took a moment for his eyes to adjust to the gloom inside the home, but once he could see, he shut the front door. He walked towards the middle of the living room and saw a large circle painted on the floor in either dark red or light brown paint. There were some strange symbols at five points around the circle, and in the center there was a collection of candles.

He crouched down to get a closer look at the circle. Could it have been drawn in blood? He wasn't sure. He could collect a chip of the paint and have it tested, but he didn't want to tamper with anything right now. No one was supposed to know he was here. He wasn't a cop anymore and there were a lot of things he wasn't legally allowed to do.

The furniture in the living room and the dining area consisted of a sofa against a far wall, a recliner, and four kitchen chairs pushed in underneath a simple wooden table.

On the walls there were more symbols similar to the ones painted around the outside of the circle on the floor. The symbols weren't familiar to him, not really resembling anything, maybe more like some kind of ancient writing.

Off of the kitchen there was a small room for a washer and dryer, but there were no appliances, only the capped-off plumbing jutting out of the wall. The tile floor had been mopped recently, maybe even scrubbed. He tried the light switch. The electricity was off.

The kitchen was clean. In a corner there was a large plastic trashcan full of garbage: empty beer and soda cans and bottles, cleaning supplies, discarded plastic bags from supermarkets, fast food takeout bags. The Formica countertops were spotless and only a battery-operated radio sat in the corner of the countertop near the corner. There were no appliances, just empty spaces between the lower cabinets where they used to be. A door at the far end of the kitchen led out to the parking area. Theron tested the door. It was locked, but he twisted the lock on the door so that it was unlocked. It would be easier to get back inside tonight if he needed to. The doorknob looked recently replaced, and he remembered Cyn telling him that Damon had changed the doorknobs and locks when they started hanging out here.

A large Igloo cooler sat on the floor where the refrigerator would have been. Theron opened it up; there was a few inches of water inside from where ice had melted. Three cans of beer sat in the water. He checked the cabinets and found supplies stocked in a few of them: bottles of aspirin and other pain relievers, a pack of Band-Aids, gauze, cloth and duct tape, a stack of CDs—all heavy metal and punk music, two battery-powered lanterns, a small pouch of tools, extra packs of C and D batteries, packs of gum and hard candy.

It bothered Theron that everything was so neat and clean, how everything had been put away in the cabinets. This hangout didn't look like drunken, reckless teenagers hung out here; this place looked cared for, like someone's home.

The bathroom at the other side of the house was clean even though the water wasn't turned on. A large plastic bucket in the bathtub was filled up with water. There were more gallons of water lined up on the sink countertop along with a battery-powered lantern and a few candles. In the medicine cabinet there was a bar of soap still in the box, a bottle of shampoo, two kinds of deodorant, a tube of toothpaste, two toothbrushes stored in plastic cases, and some dental floss.

Both bedrooms were on this side of the house. The larger one was towards the front of the house and Theron checked that one first.

A mattress was shoved into the corner on the floor with bedsheets folded up at the end of it and two pillows on top of the sheets. On the floor next to the mattress was another battery-powered CD player/radio, more candles, a few CDs and paperback books stacked up neatly. In the closet there were a few extra sets of clothes hanging from the metal rod and an empty duffel bag on the top shelf. Even the closet smelled clean.

Theron went down the short hallway to the next bedroom. He pushed the door open and then stopped cold at what he saw in there.

TWENTY-EIGHT

THERON

Theron stood in the doorway of the second room. The room was swept clean and it was empty except for a group of objects piled up in the far corner. He entered the room and walked across the chipped tiled floor towards the corner. There was a stack of new plastic tarps, blue ones, all of them still in the packaging. There was also a box of construction garbage bags, four rolls of duct tape stacked up on top of each other, a few coils of brand-new rope, and a thick steel chain with a hook at one end of it.

He had a pretty good idea what these were for.

Theron walked back out to the living room and headed for the set of French doors that led out to a back porch area—this was the only place he hadn't checked yet.

The back porch was a typical patio area of a Florida stucco home. It ran almost the whole length of the back of the home and was covered by the roof, the edge of it held up by stucco-covered columns. A knee wall coated with chipped stucco lined the far edge of the patio with an opening that would have led out to the backyard if there was one and not the jungle-like brush and trees right up next to the house. The floor was concrete and swept clean like the rest of the home. In the middle of the ceiling there was a ceiling fan, but decades of humidity had warped the fan's blades and they drooped down like a wilting flower.

In a far corner of the patio there was a collection of tools: three shovels, two metal garden rakes, a pick, a pair of large pruning shears, battery-powered hedge trimmers, and a gas-powered weed trimmer. Theron walked over to inspect the tools. Dirt coated the shovels and rakes, the dirt dusty and dry now. Dried grass and vegetation was crusted on the weed trimmer and hedge trimmer, bits of plant material clogging the teeth. All of these tools had been used recently.

He touched the butt of his gun again as he looked back at the French doors. It felt for a moment like someone was watching him. A creepy-crawling feeling danced along his skin again.

He knew what the shovels and gardening tools had been used for, and he needed to check it out. He looked at the brush and trees just beyond the back porch—it looked like a wall of impenetrable jungle. The grass and weeds were even higher than the knee wall in some places. Clouds of gnats hovered in the air and a few birds chirped from somewhere in the trees. Squirrels ran along the pine and oak tree branches and rustled through the undergrowth and dead leaves, making them sound much larger than they were. He imagined there were plenty of snakes in those woods so he grabbed one of the metal rakes and took it with him as he left the back porch and entered the woods.

He tried to be quiet as he trekked through the woods, but it was impossible not to make a sound on the carpet of dead leaves and dry grass and the weeds he crunched down with each footstep. Theron was no outdoorsman by any stretch of the imagination, but he could already tell there was a trail through the brush once he was twenty feet into the woods.

After a few minutes of walking, the trees began to thin out and then the woods opened up to a small clearing, much of the weeds, grass, and small brush cleared away with the weed trimmer and hedge trimmers. And right in the middle of the clearing was a large hole in the ground with a huge mound of dirt right beside it.

Another chill ran across Theron's skin and he wanted to draw his gun, but he gripped the handle of the rake like a weapon instead, his hands already sweating inside the latex gloves. He ventured closer to the hole in the ground.

Let's call it what it is—a grave.

He peeked over the edge of the grave and looked down into the bottom of the large hole. The grave was empty; the sides of it had been dug at angles, and some of the dirt was chopped up at the far end where the digger had crawled out of hole. Roots poked out of the sides of the grave and the dirt bottom was already littered with dead leaves. Insects and worms wriggled around among the leaves at the bottom, which still looked moist from the rain last night.

This was a grave . . . a grave for their first kill. For Ashley Lowe, the one Cyn believed had been Damon's first victim?

Or was this grave for another victim? Was it for Cyn?

Theron hurried back through the woods to the house. He knocked the dirt off of the bottom of his shoes and put the rake back among the tools in the corner of the back porch. He peered into the house through the French doors, but he didn't see anyone inside. He went around the back of the house, trudging through the weeds and grass, knocking spider webs out of the way. He stopped at the corner and peeked out at the parking area and clearing, making sure no one had come while he'd been in the woods.

No Dodge minivan. No motorcycle.

Theron returned to the back porch and entered the house through the French doors. He locked the handle on the one French door. Then he walked through the house two more times, getting the layout memorized even though it was fairly simple.

It looked like Cyn's friends still hung out here, and it looked like they would be back. It didn't seem like they were afraid that someone might tell the police about this house. Maybe Damon was sure Cyn wouldn't betray them even though she had quit the Vampire Game.

Theron stripped his gloves off as he walked back to his car, balling them up and stuffing them into his jacket pocket. He knew he was going to come back later tonight and stake this house out, see if Damon and the others showed up.

TWENTY-NINE

THERON

After leaving the abandoned house, Theron went back to his office for a few hours. It was still early and he wanted to do a little research and make a few phone calls before he went by any of Cyn's friend's houses.

When he got to his office, he went inside and locked the door. There was a chance a potential client might drop by, but not a good one. He'd already checked his voicemail, his website, and his emails. Nothing. He could focus one hundred percent of his effort on this vampire case now.

He sat down at his desk with his notes scribbled down on his little notebook. He turned his desktop computer on and looked up the warehouse where Ronnie worked. He dialed the number and a woman answered. He asked to speak to Ronnie Costas. She transferred him to an angry man.

"Ronnie doesn't work here anymore," the angry man told him.

"Was he fired?"

"Hell, yeah. He didn't show up three days in a row. No call, no show. That gets you fired. There are plenty of other people in this world that can drive a forklift."

"Did he come in for his last check or anything?"

"No. Everything's direct deposit these days."

"Do you have any idea where he might be working now?" It was a longshot, but maybe . . .

"No. Listen, I need to get back to work."

Theron hung the phone up and looked at his notes. He saw the website that Cyn had written down. He tried looking it up but he couldn't find it. Then he remembered that she'd told him it was on the dark web.

It took a few moments to sign into the dark web, and then to find the website.

The website looked exactly the same as it had last night, the title and the logo at the top of the page with the woman's red lips and fangs right under that. At the bottom of the page was the rectangle with the words ENTER CODE right above it. There was nothing else on the screen, no help or contact buttons, no sign of who had created the website. He clicked and double-clicked on everything, but nothing happened. He entered Cyn's code, but like she had predicted, nothing happened because the code was obsolete now.

Theron sighed and signed out of the vampire website. He had a little more time to kill before he made his rounds of interviews; he wanted to wait until later in the afternoon when he might catch some of them at home. He looked up message boards and other websites about vampires on the dark web.

Vampires are Real! one website proclaimed. Theron did some reading, and a lot of what the website claimed was similar to what Cyn had told him: vampires weren't the undead; they were very much alive but had been changed physically by a biological process. The author also claimed that a potential vampire had to be introduced to the virus-tainted blood little by little so not to shock the system, which could be deadly.

Theron thought of the party Cyn had told him that she and her friends had attended. He thought about the dark red wine they had drunk. Could there have been tainted blood in that wine? Just enough to introduce the virus into their systems without overwhelming them? Did that mean Cyn was part vampire whether she wanted to be one or not?

He shook his head, trying to clear his mind as he sat back in his chair. He could see the lure of the myth, the seduction of it. All of the accounts and stories—on the dark web at least—seemed to corroborate Cyn's stories about the vampires, this cabal of ancient beings who supposedly ran things behind the scenes. One website predicted the time of vampires was soon at hand— that within a decade the vampires would come out of hiding and reveal themselves once they had total control over the world.

The thought of it gave him a shudder, but then he thought of the possibility of an extended life, of the strength and power that came with being a vampire. Once again, he understood the lure of it all. Who wouldn't want that? Especially someone like him with a death sentence hanging over his head.

He looked back at his computer again and switched to the regular web. He searched for news articles about Ashley Lowe, the teenager that Cyn suspected had been Damon's first kill.

It turned out Ashley Lowe was from Lakeland. She had been missing for almost a week now. The Polk County sheriff's department had put up a reward for any information about her, and another larger reward was being offered by Ashley's family. Ashley Lowe was a pretty girl, as Cyn had said, almost as pretty as Cyn was.

Ashley had last been seen with a friend who said they had gone to a party together. The friend had lost track of Ashley, but thought she might have gone somewhere with a group of friends she had just met at the party. That was the last time anyone had seen or heard from her. Her cell phone was turned off and couldn't be tracked, like someone had taken the battery out and destroyed the phone. No trace of her. Nothing.

Theron wondered how old the photograph of Ashley was—a year old? He wondered what kind of party she had gone to. He wondered if she was into goth and vampires like Cyn and Damon were.

He shut off his computer and glanced at his cell phone, checking the time. He was surprised that two hours had slipped by. He went to his back room and warmed up another sandwich in his microwave for lunch, not the food his doctor told him he should be eating, but of course his doctor told him a healthy diet might only extend his life a few years at best. He washed his processed food and two of his heart pills down with a can of Coke.

Now it was time to make the rounds. He would drive by each of their homes, but according to Cyn there wasn't a good chance of finding any of them at home. But it was something to do at least.

THIRTY

THERON

Theron went to Mel's house first, but no one was home. No one was home at Damon's house, either—and his motorcycle wasn't in the driveway or beside the house. After Damon's house, Theron went to the rundown trailer park where Jeremy lived, but no one answered the door at the trailer. Two neighbors were hanging out on their porch. Theron walked over to them and asked about Jeremy, but the two men were close-lipped, sarcastic, and suspicious.

He got back into his car and remembered that Cyn had said that Stan, Ronnie's uncle that he shared an apartment with, was on disability and drank all night. There was a good chance he might be at home, sleeping it off.

Theron parked near the intersection of Eighth Street and Loomis Avenue in front of a large house that had been converted into three apartments. The house had probably been a fine home decades ago, but it had deteriorated along with the neighborhood around it.

An older lady sat on the sagging front porch. She smoked a cigarette and sat in a rocking chair, slowly rocking back and forth, staring at Theron as he approached. The table next to her was littered with beer cans, overflowing ashtrays, wads of paper and other trash. There was a rotting porch swing at the other end of the porch, suspended by rusty lengths of chain. Dead and wilted plants drooped in a few pots near the front door, which was wide open with only a screen door on a wooden frame keeping the gnats and flies out of the house. A baby cried somewhere inside the house and a dog barked nonstop from a nearby backyard.

"Hello, ma'am," Theron said as he climbed the spongy wooden steps up to the front porch.

The woman didn't respond. She sucked in more smoke from her cigarette, blew it back out slowly, still rocking in her chair.

"I'm trying to find Ronnie Costas. He lives at this address with his Uncle Stan."

The woman nodded and pointed towards the other end of the porch, the burning cigarette held delicately between two skeletal fingers. "They live in the apartment above the garage," she said in a creaky voice. "There's a set of stairs on the other side of the garage."

"Thank you, ma'am."

The woman said nothing. The baby still hadn't stopped crying and the dog hadn't stopped barking.

Theron found the set of wooden steps on the other side of the garage and they looked even more unsafe than the front porch. He took each step gingerly as he made his way carefully up to the second floor deck. The deck was small with nothing on it, the wood gray with petrification and dry rot; the railings were warped and dotted with faded bird droppings. Theron knocked on the door.

"Who is it?" a man called from inside the apartment. That couldn't be Ronnie's voice—it had to be Stan. The door had a small window in it, but it was covered on the inside with a curtain.

Theron knocked again, pounding on the door—that incessant police knock that got people's attention, a knock that said he wasn't going away anytime soon.

"Who is it?" the man said from inside, but he was closer now, right on the other side of the door.

"My name is Theron Metcalf. I'm trying to find Ronnie Costas."

No answer from the other side of the door. Theron could practically hear Ronnie's uncle thinking about what to do.

"Are you Stan Costas?"

No answer again for a moment, and then: "You a cop?"

"I'm a friend of Cynthia Byers. I think Ronnie calls her Cyn."

"Ronnie's not here. Come back later."

"Do you know where I can find him?"

"He hasn't been here for a few days. I don't know where the hell he is."

Theron felt like he was losing this battle. He knew that Stan was going to walk away at any moment and not come back to the door. "I called the warehouse where Ronnie works. They said he was fired."

Another long pause from Stan. Theron suspected that Ronnie's termination from his job was news to Stan.

"I'm also trying to find Ronnie's friends, Damon and Jeremy."

"What do you want Ronnie for?" Stan asked. He was still close to the door.

"I just need to talk to him."

"Come back later. I don't know where to find him."

Again Theron felt the fear that Stan was done talking and that he was going to walk away. He felt a moment of desperation and blurted out his next question: "Sir, do you know anything about the Vampire Game?"

THIRTY-ONE

THERON

There was another long moment of silence from behind the apartment door. Theron hadn't heard Stan walk away yet.

"Why do you want to know about that?" Stan asked—his voice was low, but Theron could hear him clearly.

"Could we just talk for a minute? Could you just open the door?"

The curtain moved from behind the window, and an old man's face peered out at Theron, studying him for a moment, trying to look beyond him to see if anyone else was out there. The curtain fell back over the window and the locks turned in the door. A moment later, Stan opened the door.

Stan was so thin he looked malnourished, and his skin had a sickly, yellowish tint to it. He wore a pair of gray workpants that had stains on them and a hole in one of the knees. His wife beater tank top revealed his boney body. Tufts of gray hair poked out from the collar of his shirt and out of his armpits. The hair on his head was almost completely gone, just wild patches above his ears. He had a long narrow face and he was missing a few of his front teeth. He gestured for Theron to come inside.

The apartment was small and smelled like old clothes, beer farts, and mold. The countertops were completely cluttered with dirty dishes, beer cans and bottles, empty wine bottles, takeout bags and wrappers, paper plates and bowls stacked up with food still stuck in them. Tiny fruit flies and gnats fluttered around the dirty dishes and the sink.

The living room was dingy, cramped, and claustrophobic. Magazines, newspapers, clothes, and more garbage was stacked up on the floor. The sofa was shoved against the wall with a recliner right next to it. The table in between the two pieces of furniture and the coffee table was littered with more cans, bottles, empty food packages, and plates and cups. A flat screen TV on the wall opposite of the couch was the only thing that looked new in the apartment.

As Theron stepped inside and closed the door, Stan went to the refrigerator to grab a can of beer. He didn't offer one to Theron. He walked to the TV and turned the sound down, but he didn't shut it off. He plopped down in the lumpy recliner that leaned a little to the left. The sofa had bedsheets and pillows on it, obviously the place where the man slept. Theron grabbed one of the chairs from the kitchen table and brought it five steps into the living room.

"Sorry," Stan said, nodding at the couch as he popped his can of beer open. "I sleep out here in the living room. I gave Ronnie the bedroom when we first moved in."

"You really don't know where Ronnie is?" Theron asked as he sat down on the kitchen chair.

"Why are you looking for him? You a cop? If you're a cop and I ask you, then you have to tell me. It's the law."

"I'm not a cop," Theron said and left it at that.

Stan didn't seem entirely satisfied with Theron's answer, but he didn't push the issue any further.

"What can you tell me about the Vampire Game?" Theron asked Stan.

Stan took a long sip from his beer. "You'll have to excuse me. I'm still trying to wake up."

Theron didn't say anything; he just waited for the man to continue.

"I sleep during the day now," Stan explained. "I try to stay awake most of the night."

Theron still didn't say anything; he figured he would just let the old man ramble a bit.

"Ronnie's a good kid. He's a hard worker. He doesn't get in any trouble. Maybe he's not the brightest bulb in the pack, but he's a good kid." Another swallow of beer. "But when he met that Damon kid—"

"Damon Kurtz?"

"I don't know his last name. He rides a bike. Not a Harley, one of those Japanese bikes. He's about nineteen or twenty years old, I think. Tall and thin. Long hair. And he looks . . . he looks evil. Thinks he's some kind of vampire or something. I think he's a devil worshipper. He came by a few times in the last year or so. He hangs out with another kid, a muscular kid that hardly ever wears a shirt. There were two girls with them the last time they were all here. High school girls, I think. One of them was pretty. The other one . . ." Stan let his words trail off, teetering a hand back and forth.

"What did they do when they were here? Hang out? Party?"

"I don't know. Ronnie's twenty-two years old. If he wants to drink, I don't care. As long as he doesn't drive, and as long as he shows up for work. I went to work every day until . . . well, I'm on disability now."

"Did Ronnie get into this vampire culture with Damon?"

"I think so. I mean he didn't run out and get everything pierced and tattooed like that Damon kid, or start dressing all in black, but he changed in a lot of ways. His attitude changed. He got meaner. Snapped at me more often. And the way he looked at me, like he was suddenly better than me."

Theron thought of Cyn telling him about Damon's speeches and how the rest of humanity was cattle for the superior vampires. He guessed that Ronnie might be adopting that philosophy. "Are you frightened of Damon?"

Stan's face turned a little red. Theron thought the old man was going to erupt in anger. Theron guessed that if it had been later in the evening and Stan had more alcohol running through his veins, he might've tried to protect his ego by lying about his fear of Damon, but now, with only half a beer inside of him, Stan told the truth. "That kid is creepy. There's something wrong with him."

Theron just nodded.

"And there are more of them now."

That took Theron by surprise. "What do you mean by that?"

"Yeah, I saw them about two weeks ago. That's why I've been staying awake all night. I've seen them outside by the street, standing near the streetlamp. Just watching the house."

"You don't think it could have been Damon out there?" Theron asked. He had a sudden sense of déjà vu, realizing that he had asked Cyn the same question less than twenty-four hours ago.

"I thought it might be Damon at first, but the guy I saw was taller. His shoulders were wider. I think the guy's hair might have been shorter. But that's about all I could tell. It was like the guy was just a black shadow out there in the dark. Like a shadow that had come alive. Next time I see one of them standing out there, I'm calling the cops. And I'm gonna tell Ronnie to tell those guys to stay away from here. I don't want nothing to do with them."

They were quiet for a moment while Stan drained the rest of his can of beer. Theron was sure Stan was itching to get another one now.

"Why do you really want to talk to Ronnie?" Stan asked.

"It's not Ronnie I'm after. I want to talk to Damon."

"Why?"

"I'm a private investigator. I'm working for someone."

"I thought you said you weren't a cop."

Theron didn't bother explaining the difference.

"Well, I can't tell you anything more than I already told you. I don't know where those kids go, what they do. And like I told you, Ronnie hasn't been around for three or four days now."

Theron stood up and took his chair back to the kitchen. "Thank you for talking with me."

Stan got up, standing in front of his leaning recliner. He looked older to Theron now, frailer. And he looked scared. "You be careful around Damon. He's bad news. I worked construction for years, and I was in the army for four years before that. I've lived in some of the worst neighborhoods and drank in some of the worst dive bars all my life. I've seen plenty of bad people in my life, and Damon's one of them."

Theron nodded, but he didn't thank Stan for the advice.

"And you watch out for those other ones, too—the ones I saw standing outside. I know they're tied up in all of this vampire crap those kids are into."

Theron thought so, too.

THIRTY-TWO

THERON

It was still early in the afternoon and Theron decided to go to Mel's house again. She lived in a very nice area of older homes with sprawling lawns. He parked in the driveway and rang the doorbell. He waited a few minutes, but no one came to the door. There was only one other car in the driveway. It was possible that Mel's parents were still working, or maybe out with friends. Maybe someone was home but didn't feel like answering the door.

He went back to Jeremy's trailer park and parked on the street in front of Jeremy's trailer. An older, skinny woman with a lot of makeup answered the door. A cigarette hung out of the corner of her mouth. Her heavily made-up eyes narrowed immediately when she saw a man in a suit and tie outside of her trailer, her guard up instantly.

"Is Jeremy Shaw here?"

The woman sighed, blowing out cigarette smoke at the same time. "What's he done now?"

"Are you his mother?"

"Are you a cop?"

"No, I'm not a cop."

The woman just nodded like she wasn't about to fall for that one.

"Is Jeremy here?"

"He hasn't been here for at least four days."

A man's voice shouted something from somewhere inside the trailer. She turned and yelled at him to wait a minute.

Theron pulled out his cell phone and pretended to scroll through it. "Do you know where I can find someone named Damon Kurtz? I believe he's a friend of Jeremy's."

"I don't know anything about Damon or where Jeremy is." She slammed the door shut on Theron before she said anything she felt might incriminate her.

Theron walked back to his car, feeling the weight of the other trailer park denizens watching him. He knew he was running the risk of Stan or Jeremy's mother contacting Damon or the others and letting them know that a suit was coming around and asking questions. But then again, it didn't seem like either one of those two were very close to Damon.

As he drove to Damon's house, he saw that he had an email from Harris. He pulled into a fast food drive-thru for an early dinner. He got a sandwich and a drink and then parked in a space near the back of the parking lot. He ate his cheeseburger as he scrolled through the email.

In the counties that Theron had requested there had been eleven missing people reported in the last week and a half. There had also been five murders. He checked the murders first. Two people murdered in Hillsborough County, one in Pinellas County, one in Polk County, and one in Pasco County; these four were the most populated counties of the seven that Theron had asked Harris to check. Three of the murders were gunshot victims, all of them young men, most likely drug deals or gang violence. The murder in Polk County had been a bar fight, a man stabbed in the abdomen multiple times; he died later at the hospital. The murder in Pasco County had been a domestic dispute—husband shoots wife.

The missing people from those seven counties had been mostly the usual: four teenage runaways, two elderly people who seemed to have just wandered off, and two kids abducted by a parent. There was also a man who had gone fishing in alligator-infested waters by himself and had vanished (the boat had been found but his body was gone; the incident would probably be listed as a boating accident rather than an alligator attack—wouldn't want to hurt Florida's tourism in any way). Two homeless people had also been reported missing, and that seemed a little odd, but Theron knew that little effort was going to be put into searching for them.

Of the eleven reported missing, only three of them were in Citrus County and Hernando County, and there were no murders in the last week and a half in those two counties. Two of the three missing were children most likely abducted by their fathers, and there was a teenage runaway in Citrus County.

And of course there was Ashley Lowe, the missing teenager from Polk County.

Four teenage runaways in a week and a half seemed like a lot to Theron. He wondered if this was a normal statistic for this area of Florida.

Cyn seemed sure that Ashley Lowe had been their first kill. If that was true, then Damon and his friends would've had to have traveled down to Polk County to get her. They would've had to have known about the party she had attended—the place where she was seen last—or maybe they had stumbled upon the party. Or maybe they had just driven around until they came across Ashley or some other teenager.

Maybe they had gone somewhere else to find their first kill, maybe down to Hillsborough County, or even to another county that Theron hadn't even looked at, like Orange County. Or maybe they had gone all the way over to the east coast.

Theron wrote a quick email back to Harris, thanking him for the information. He started his car, backed out of the parking space and headed for Damon's house.

THIRTY-THREE

THERON

Theron parked in the street in front of Damon's house. There was a dark blue car parked in the driveway, some kind of Chevy, but there was no motorcycle anywhere that Theron could see. He got out and looked up and down the street. It was a nice middle-class neighborhood of stucco homes and St. Augustine lawns. Two boys were tossing a football back and forth down the street.

He walked up to the front door and rang the doorbell. A moment later a slender woman dressed in nurse's scrubs answered the door. Her blond hair was tied up in a bun and she looked tired.

"Ms. Kurtz, my name is Theron Metcalf. I was wondering if I could speak to Damon."

"Damon's not here. Who are you again?"

"I'm a private investigator." Theron handed her a business card that he had plucked from an inside pocket of his suitcoat. "I'm working on a case for someone, and I just wanted to ask Damon a few questions."

She forced a smile on her face, but the suspiciousness still showed in her eyes. "Yeah. He's not here right now."

"Do you know how I could get a hold of him?"

She scrunched her face up a little like she was pretending to be thinking about it. "Uh, no. Not really."

"Does he work somewhere?"

The suspiciousness turned into full guard now. "He, uh . . . he helps his friend Jeremy. They do some kind of construction stuff or lawn work, I think."

"I see," Theron said, nodding. He knew it was a lie, but maybe it was a lie Damon told his mother and she believed it. He wasn't going to challenge her on it.

"Is Damon in some sort of trouble?" she asked.

"I just wanted to talk to him. Have the police been by to see you?"

"Look, I'm not going to answer any of your questions."

Ms. Kurtz was close to closing the door now, and there was nothing Theron would be able to do to stop her. Again, out of desperation, he decided to use the same tactic he had used on Ronnie's uncle. "Has Damon ever talked about something called The Vampire Game?"

Ms. Kurtz didn't say anything for a few seconds, but Theron could see her anger building. "My son happens to like vampire movies and books. What is The Vampire Game, some kind of role-playing game or something?"

"I don't know. I've just heard it mentioned a few times, and I was wondering if you knew anything about it."

"No."

"Has Damon been home in the last few days?"

"He's an adult. He can come and go when he pleases. Who are you working for?"

"I really can't say."

"It's Cyn, isn't it? Damon told me that he broke up with her, and now she's stalking him."

"She's been stalking *him*?" Theron asked with a smile.

"Is that so impossible to believe?"

"It's just I heard it might be the other way around."

Ms. Kurtz's face flushed red. "My son is a good kid. But that Cyn . . . well, let's just say she's great at manipulating people. And now she's manipulated you, she's got you running all over town for her. You need to be careful with her."

Theron could tell that Ms. Kurtz was going to defend her son to hell and back whether he was guilty or not. This was a no-win situation for him now, and it was probably time to cut his losses and move on to something else.

Besides, he was just doing some legwork while waiting for the night to come so he could go back out to the abandoned house.

"I'm sorry to have bothered you," Theron said.

Ms. Kurtz slammed the door shut. Theron walked to his car without a look back at the house. He was sure Ms. Kurtz was watching him leave, making sure he got in his car and drove away.

Somewhere deep down inside, Ms. Kurtz knew the truth about her son, that he wasn't the good boy that she believed he was. He wondered how many people Ms. Kurtz had driven out of her life in defense of her son through the years: husbands, boyfriends, family, friends, neighbors. Now she was a woman alone in her house; her son she adored had abandoned her. One day she would wake up in tears and realize that Damon had never truly loved her like she had loved him, that all of his affections had been contrived to control her.

THIRTY-FOUR

THERON

Theron pulled up in front of Cyn's home. There was only one car parked in the driveway, a silver Volvo.

He parked his car in the street and got out. He looked up and down the street, but everything was pretty quiet—this neighborhood seemed like a working-class area, and most people around here were probably still at work. The street wasn't very busy and no one was outside on their porches or in their front yards. He looked across the street at the line of streetlights up and down the sidewalk, picking out the area where Damon must have been standing when Cyn had seen him two nights ago.

Cyn's home was a modest, one-story stucco house, painted gray with dark trim. There was a little front porch and a small side yard beyond the driveway, and just beyond the side yard was the wooden fence with a gate right in the middle of it.

He went to the front door and rang the doorbell. He didn't hear the sound of the doorbell from inside, but he waited thirty seconds before knocking. He waited a few more seconds and knocked again, rapping harder.

Nobody came to the door.

It was already late afternoon. Cyn had told him that her mom did some work from home, but it didn't seem like anyone was home. School should've been out and Cyn's sisters should've been home by now. Or Cyn should've at least been home.

Theron pulled his cell phone out and dialed Cyn's number. It rang five times and then went to voicemail.

"Hey, Cyn," Theron said into the phone as he walked towards the driveway. "It's Theron. I just wanted to call you and let you know what I've found out so far. Call me back when you get this."

He hung up the phone as he walked to the gate in the fence. He thumbed the little black lever on the door, but it was locked from the inside. He tried to peek over the top of the fence, but it was too tall.

What did he expect to find anyway? The cops had already been here. They hadn't found any footprints or signs that Damon had been there the other night.

He walked to his car, glancing inside the Volvo's windows as he passed it. Instead of getting in his car, he walked across the street to the sidewalk, to where he thought Damon might have been standing, and then he turned around and stared at Cyn's house for a moment.

"Can I help you with something?"

Theron turned around. An old lady was shuffling towards him from her house, hurrying down her walkway towards him even though she had to be at least eighty years old.

"Oh, I'm sorry, ma'am," Theron said, smiling at her. "I was just trying to see if the Byers family was home."

The old woman stopped at the end of her walkway that connected with the sidewalk. The lawn on each side of the walkway was a green carpet of St. Augustine grass, and the shrubs and plants decorating the front of her home were tidy. She stared at Theron.

Theron pulled out his wallet and flipped it open, showing the woman his P.I. badge which, from a distance, resembled a police badge. "I'm working for the Byers family, investigating an incident that occurred here a few nights ago."

"You mean the man who was standing out here on the sidewalk?"

"Yes. Did you see him?"

"Oh yes, I saw him."

"Do you remember when that was?"

She cocked her head a little as she thought it over. "I think it was about two nights ago, like you just said. Sometime around two or three o'clock in the morning. I don't sleep too well these days." She smiled. "When you get to be my age, you sleep a few hours here and a few hours there. You take sleep when you can get it."

Theron nodded patiently. "What exactly did you see that night, ma'am?"

"Oh, just call me Martha."

"Martha."

"Well, like I said, I was up and I looked out my front windows and saw a man standing out here on the sidewalk."

"What did this man look like?"

"It was dark, and he was standing far enough away from the streetlight so that I couldn't really see him too well. But I remember he had this long coat on. He seemed to be dressed all in black. And he had long hair. I remember that. His hair, it was blowing around in the wind a little. At first I thought he was looking right at me, and I had quite a fright." She chuckled.

Theron smiled along with her. "I can imagine."

"But then I realized that he was turned the other way. He was looking across the street."

"At the Byers' home?"

She nodded. "Yes."

"Did you call the police about this?"

"You know, I was going to. But then I decided not to. I mean, the man was just standing on the sidewalk. He wasn't in my yard, and he wasn't doing anything wrong. But I decided to watch him, make sure that he didn't come in my yard. But I looked away for just a second, and he was gone."

"Gone?"

"Yes. It was the strangest thing. I looked away, at my cat—she was hissing like the dickens—and when I looked back out through the window, the man was gone. I figured I was still half-asleep, or I hadn't gotten enough sleep. I thought I might have been, you know . . ."

"Seeing things?" Theron offered.

She nodded. "It's a real fear at my age. It was either that or . . ." Again, she let her words trail off.

"Or?"

"Or I thought I had seen a ghost."

A chill danced along Theron's skin. He thought about the man he'd seen in the Dairy Queen parking lot last night, the one who had been there one moment and then gone the next.

"So, you see," the old lady continued, "I just felt strange calling the police and telling them I thought I saw a man on the sidewalk. I would sound like some nutty old woman, so I just locked my doors and stayed awake the rest of the night. But when I saw you out here, standing here, I thought maybe you were looking into it."

"Yes, ma'am. We think the man was Cynthia Byers' ex-boyfriend. They just broke up and he's been doing a little bit of stalking. I'm sure it's nothing to worry about."

Relief flooded the woman's face. "Good. I don't try to get in my neighbors' business."

"Of course not, but I appreciate you talking to me about this. It helps more than you know."

The old woman beamed. "Well, I'm glad I could help."

Theron was about to walk back to his car, but he turned and looked at the old woman again, smiling at her. "You didn't happen to see the cops at the Byers' home a few nights ago, did you? The night before you saw the man standing out here on the sidewalk?"

"No. I don't remember seeing the police, but I may have slept through it. Like I said, I have to take sleep when I can get it."

"So the police never came by and asked you about the man you saw standing in front of your house?"

She shook her head. "No. You're the first one I've talked to about it."

Theron smiled at her. "Thank you, Martha."

"You're very welcome," she said.

Theron turned and walked across the street to his car.

THIRTY-FIVE

THERON

The old woman watched Theron from her front lawn as he got back into his car. His cell phone rang as soon as he shut the car door. It was Cyn.

"Cyn," Theron said as he answered the phone.

"Sorry. I just got your message. I stayed after school today to make up some schoolwork."

"I thought you said you weren't going to school right now with all of this going on."

"I've already missed a few days. I've got a lot of work to make up."

The car was running, but Theron still hadn't pulled away from the front of Cyn's house yet. He looked across the street at Martha as she walked back to her house. "I went by your house today," he told Cyn.

There was a moment of silence from Cyn. "You did? When?"

He could hear the alarm in her voice even though she was trying to hide it. "Just a little while ago," Theron said. A little white lie since he was still parked in front of her home. "No one was home."

"My dad's probably still at work. My mom took my sisters up to my grandma's house in Ohio for the week until all of this . . . this stuff with Damon gets resolved. They're all pretty scared."

"Why didn't you go with them?"

"Because I need to help stop this. I helped start this, helped cause this. I'm partly responsible."

Theron didn't know what to say to that. He glanced across the street again, watching Martha enter her home. "I talked to a neighbor of yours who lives across the street. Her name's Martha."

"I don't know any of our neighbors very well."

"She said she saw Damon standing on the sidewalk in front of her home two nights ago. She saw him watching your house around two o'clock in the morning."

Cyn sighed into the phone. "You still don't believe me, do you?"

"I didn't say that."

"But you feel the need to question my neighbors, corroborating my story. I showed you the picture I took of Damon standing on the sidewalk that night. I'm not lying about this."

"I believe you, Cyn."

"I don't think you do. And I think you're underestimating how dangerous Damon and the others really are."

Theron didn't feel like getting into an argument with his client—it wasn't usually good for business. He wanted to change the subject. "Look, it's getting late. I'm going out to the abandoned house now. I'm going to stake the place out. See if Damon and the rest of them come by. I want to see if they're bringing someone with them."

"Like their first kill? Like Ashley Lowe?"

"Yeah. I want to be there at that house tonight. I've talked with Ronnie's uncle, and I talked with Damon's mother and Jeremy's mother. I didn't really get anywhere with any of them. Either they don't know where Damon and his friends are, or they don't want to tell me. But I have a feeling that Damon and his friends might be going back to that house tonight."

"What makes you think that?"

"I was out there this morning. The place looks like a hangout, except it's really clean."

"Yeah, Damon wanted the place clean all the time." Cyn was quiet for a moment. "So that's what makes you think they're going back out there tonight, because the place is clean?"

Theron still hadn't put his car in drive. "No, there's something else that makes me think they're going there tonight."

"What?"

"Look, Cyn. I know it's probably been a few weeks since you've been to that house, but I need to tell you something about it."

She was silent. Theron imagined that she was bracing herself. "Okay," she whispered.

"I found some shovels and other tools on the back porch. And in the spare bedroom I found brand new tarps, garbage bags, duct tape, rope, and a long chain."

"See? I told you I'm not making this up. I told you they're planning their first kill."

"That's not all I found. The shovels had dirt on them. I found a trail in the woods behind the house. About two or three hundred feet into the woods, there's a clearing. Someone dug a grave there. It was empty when I saw it this morning, waiting to be filled in."

"Oh my God," Cyn whispered.

"Yeah. I wasn't going to tell you, but I felt like I should warn you."

"Believe me, I'm already scared enough."

Theron was about to put his car into drive, but he waited a moment longer. "Are you sure you're going to be alright here at your house?"

Silence on the phone again for a moment. "Yeah. I think Damon wanted me for his first kill, but I think they had no choice but to go after someone else first. Remember, there's a time limit that each task has to be done by. If they couldn't get to me, then they had to get to someone else before the time ran out."

"Like Ashley Lowe?" Theron suggested.

"Or even someone else."

"Okay. I'm going to the abandoned house for the rest of the night. I want you to make sure you're with your dad at all times. I don't want you going anywhere by yourself."

"My dad's coming to pick me up at school. Then we'll probably go get something to eat."

"Good. Try to stay out as long as you can. And make sure you have your cell phone with you at all times. You need to be careful."

"You need to be careful, too," Cyn said. "It will be dark soon. They are more powerful at night."

"I can handle it." There was one more thing Theron had to tell her. "Look, I can't go to the cops with what I have right now. You understand that, don't you? I'm just a civilian now; I don't have any authority to be snooping around an abandoned property. I don't even have enough evidence to do anything with."

"What about the grave?"

"Right now that's just a hole in the ground. I need to be careful about this. The only way we're going to nab these guys is if I catch them in the act. If we spook them, if we tip them off somehow, they'll run, and we might not find them again before . . ." He let his words trail off.

"Before they get someone else," Cyn finished and then sighed into the phone. It sounded like a shudder. "I'm not going to talk to any of them, if that's what you think. I'm through with them."

"Okay."

"If you see Damon at that house tonight, or anyone else out there at that house, you just need to call the police," Cyn told him. "Don't try to do anything by yourself."

"I'll be okay. Just keep your cell phone on the whole time in case I need to get a hold of you."

"I will."

"And remember, if you see Damon and the others, just call the police," Cyn said.

"I will," Theron said and then hung up his phone. But he had no intentions of calling the police if he saw Damon—he had other plans for them tonight.

THIRTY-SIX

THERON

The sun was low on the horizon as Theron drove down Allen Road towards the abandoned house. The setting sun painted the sky with reds, oranges, and yellows, a blazing inferno—the day dying and making way for the night.

After stopping on the wooded trail to open the metal gate, Theron got back in his car and drove through so he could close the gate and wrap the chain around it again. A surprisingly cold wind had kicked up with the coming darkness. A cold front must be swooping down from the north, but Theron hadn't looked at the weather report on his phone in the last two days. He hadn't brought an extra coat with him, so his suitcoat would have to do.

He idled down the dirt drive towards the house hidden in the trees and brush in the distance. He kept his headlights off and his car was just a dark object creeping down the driveway, the engine of his car practically silent. There was a chance Damon or some of the others could already be at the house, but he didn't think so.

As he pulled up closer to the house, Theron didn't see any other vehicles in the parking area next to the house or in the clearing. There were too many trees and brush to hide any cars or trucks behind the house . . . maybe a motorcycle, but that would be it.

Theron rolled down his window and stared at the house for a moment. He didn't see any signs of candlelight inside, but someone could be hiding in the dark inside the house. He got out of the car, but left the engine running. He felt the reassuring weight of his gun in his shoulder holster as he walked towards the house. He went around the back to make sure Damon hadn't stashed his bike there.

No motorcycle behind the house.

He thought about checking the grave in the woods, but there would be plenty of time for that later.

Everything was silent except for the crickets beginning to chirp. A few bats flew across the dark blue sky, and the last remnants of daylight were splashed across the western horizon. The twilight seemed suddenly ominous to Theron, like the light was fading fast and the darkness would last forever after that.

He shook his head a little, trying to shake out those strange thoughts and that eerie feeling that had risen up inside of him so quickly. He got back in his car and drove around the stands of shrubs and brush off to the left of the clearing, the hiding place he'd found for his car when he'd been here this morning.

After parking, Theron shut his car off. He had already turned off the dome light so if he needed to open his car door later, the light wouldn't come on. He settled back into the driver's seat, trying to get comfortable. He had his thermos with him and he had filled it with coffee at a gas station store before driving out here. He had also bought a twelve-pack of Mountain Dew—it was on the floorboard in the back of the car. This could be a long night.

They might not even come to this house tonight.

And why would they? Obviously they were laying low now, sure that the police might be looking for them.

But there was that empty grave in the woods—they would come back to fill it. No, Theron was sure they were coming tonight.

As he sat there, some of the things Cyn had said were beginning to bother him a little. He recalled his conversation with Damon's mother, how she had said that Cyn was a manipulator. Cyn had manipulated Damon, that's what Ms. Kurtz had said.

Theron wondered if Cyn might have been lying about some things. Some of these details weren't adding up.

He closed his eyes, wondering if he should give Harris at the police station another call, ask him about the police reports, the times when the police had come out to Cyn's house. But he didn't want to involve the police—he had other plans.

He was tired. He hadn't slept much in the last two nights. He kept his eyes closed as his thoughts turned to vampires and the research he had done earlier in the day. He wondered what it would be like to be a vampire. There were so many reports of people on the dark web talking about vampires, and their stories all seemed so similar. Wouldn't it be strange to find out that a race of people had existed for centuries but managed to stay in the shadows? Wouldn't it be strange if the vampires had even propagated some of the myths to hide their true nature? He fantasized for a moment what it would be like to have an immune system like that; something so powerful that it could heal all ailments and conquer any new diseases or injuries. He fantasized about the strength and the power. He wondered what it would be like to be part of a secret brotherhood like that, a cabal that had unshakable devotion to each other.

He drifted off to sleep without even realizing it, his thoughts turning into dreams. He dreamed of a party in a mansion by the bay. There were pale, beautiful women there, swaying to music. The women had fangs and blood-red lips.

But then his dream shifted to a huge conference room high up in an office building. A gigantic mahogany table took up the center of the massive room with sixteen men seated around it. These were the CEOs, governors, and intelligence directors from around the world—some of the most powerful people in the world, men dressed in thousand-dollar business suits.

Theron hovered somewhere up in the corner of the room, floating near the ceiling, watching the men from that height as they talked and debated, as they made decisions that affected millions of people with the stroke of a pen. The men argued a little, but it never got out of control; there were disagreements in some cases, but everything remained amiable.

He heard a motorcycle from somewhere outside the conference room. The huge double doors flew open and a motorcycle sped inside the room, the rider dressed entirely in black with a full-faced helmet that hid his features. The man rode the bike around the room, circling the table, the bike's headlight splashing around the room.

As the headlight flashed across the walls, Theron noticed that there were symbols on the walls, all of them painted in bright red blood. He hadn't noticed those symbols before. There was also a big circle painted in blood right in the middle of the table, a group of candles gathered together right in the center of the circle. There were more symbols painted on the table, one in front of each person seated at the table.

The men around the table watched the biker with interest, but they didn't seem afraid of him, or even upset that he had interrupted their important business.

The bike stopped and the rider sat back, straddling his bike as it idled. He took his helmet off.

It was Damon.

Theron's eyes popped open in the darkness. For just a second he couldn't remember where he was—his sleep had been that deep. He heard the sound of a motorcycle coming from somewhere out in the darkness.

It was all coming back to him now. He was in his car, parked behind some brush and trees, hidden from the abandoned house. He was waiting for Damon and his crew to show up.

And now Damon was here.

THIRTY-SEVEN

THERON

Theron waited twenty minutes before getting out of his car. The motorcycle had shut off long ago. Right after the motorcycle, he had heard the sound of another motor, some kind of vehicle; Mel's minivan, it had to be. After the engines were shut off, Theron heard them talking in the dark, laughing and shouting at each other. They didn't seem nervous; they didn't seem like people hiding from the cops.

Moments later their laughter and talking faded away as they went inside the house.

Theron slipped on a pair of black latex gloves as he waited. He guessed Damon and the others would be in the house for a while. Had they brought someone with them? There hadn't been a sense of urgency or nervousness in their voices that Theron would've heard from people transporting a victim or a dead body. But then again, they were vampires, they were confident in what they were doing.

Theron got out of his car and closed the door softly. He made himself wait another two minutes after gently closing the door. He listened for any sounds in the dark as he checked his gun, making sure it was snug in the shoulder holster. He also made sure he had his cell phone with him. He would need both of these for his plan to work.

He crept from the bushes, and then hurried across the clearing to Mel's van. He waited behind her van for a moment, peeking in the windows. No one inside. He looked at the house. There was the slightest flickering of light coming from the living room windows. They were in there, they were doing something. Another ritual? Another task to get them closer to becoming vampires? Planning their next kill?

Theron ran from Mel's van to the parking area next to the house and then to the door that led into the kitchen. He'd left this door unlocked when he'd been here earlier, but they could've checked the doors when they got here and locked it. Of course, if they had found a door unlocked, they might suspect that someone had been snooping around inside the house earlier.

Paranoid thoughts crept into Theron's mind. Had he disturbed anything when he'd been here earlier? Had he moved something slightly? Had he left some kind of sign that he'd been here? Had he left minute amounts of dirt on the floor after he'd come back from the woods?

Were their senses heightened? Could they smell his scent or feel his presence from when he'd been in the house earlier? Could they even sense him out here right now?

He wrapped his gloved hand around the doorknob and twisted it so slowly, soundlessly.

It was still unlocked.

He pushed the door open inch by inch, praying that it wouldn't creak. But the door was silent and Theron slipped inside the kitchen. He kept his eyes on the archway to the living room as he eased the door shut again. One candle burned at the other end of the kitchen, closer to the archway. The candle was on the countertop right beside the battery-powered radio. More candlelight came from the living room, the light flickering off the walls of the dining area that he could see from where he stood.

Damon and the others were deeper in the living room, sitting around the circle on the floor, Theron supposed. He could hear them talking. Four of them: three males and one female. They were talking too low for Theron to make out everything they were saying. They were talking fast, but not arguing with each other, but it sounded like they were definitely discussing something important. Theron thought of his dream about the men around the boardroom table, discussing things vehemently but not arguing.

Were they nervous? Excited? The tone of their voices could have meant either one.

Theron moved silently through the kitchen, getting closer to the archway. He pulled his gun out of his holster, gripping it in his gloved hand as he peeked around the corner of the archway. All four of them were seated on the floor around the circle just like he had suspected: Damon, Jeremy, Mel, and Ronnie. The group of candles in the middle of the circle burned brightly, providing enough light to illuminate the whole living room.

Damon wore his long trench coat, the coat splayed around him as he sat cross-legged on the floor in front of the circle, his back towards the archway that led to the two bedrooms and the bathroom. Above their circle, dangling from the ceiling was the length of chain Theron had seen in the bedroom, one end wrapped around an exposed rafter. Mel was dressed in tight-fitting, black clothing, and judging from the photos he had seen of her, it looked like she had lost a lot of weight; her body was toned and tightened now. Jeremy wore a black sleeveless shirt, showing off his muscled arms. Ronnie was dressed all in black like the others. He looked more confident now, and he didn't have his glasses on. Maybe he didn't need them anymore.

Theron needed to act quickly; he wanted to listen to them and try to make out what they were whispering about, but he couldn't risk the chance that one of them might get up and split away from the group—he needed all of them to stay together. It was time to act while he could still take them by surprise.

Theron charged out of the archway with his gun aimed at the four of them. "Don't move!"

The four looked at Theron with shock, their faces frozen, eyes wide. Ronnie even raised his hands up a little in surrender.

Theron loved the shock on their faces, loved the fear he could feel coming from them. They were powerful, sure, but not *too* powerful yet.

"Who the hell are you?" Damon asked with a scowl.

"Doesn't matter," Theron said. "All you need to know right now is that if you move an inch you're getting a bullet between your eyes."

"You think a bullet can kill us?" Damon asked, the ghost of a smile beginning to form.

Theron glanced from Damon to each of the others. They all seemed to be relaxing a little now, all of them smiling. Ronnie had lowered his hands back down into his lap.

"Yes, I think bullets can kill you," Theron said. "I know your secrets. I know you're strong and you can heal quickly, but I know you're not immortal. I know there are some injuries you can't heal from fast enough—like a bullet to the brain."

Damon's smile slipped just a bit.

Theron pulled his cell phone out as he moved towards the small wooden dining table with the chairs around it, keeping his gun aimed at them the entire time. None of them had moved an inch yet. "I want the code to the Vampire Game," he told them. He already had the Vampire Game website pulled up on his phone with the keyboard at the bottom of the screen so he could enter the code.

Damon stared at Theron. "You want to be a vampire? Is that it?"

"I want that code," Theron repeated.

"You want the healing power?" Damon asked. "You want the strength, the speed, the power? The knowledge? The secrets of the world?"

"I want it all," Theron said.

"I don't know if I can give you the code," Damon said with a frown. "I don't know if I'm allowed to do that. I don't know if that's against the rules."

"I don't care. I want that code."

Damon cocked his head slightly in an exaggerated gesture of thinking Theron's request over for a moment. "What if I don't?" Damon finally asked. "You kill me? Is that it? You definitely won't get the code then."

Theron aimed his gun at Mel, then at Jeremy. "Maybe I'll kill the ones closest to you."

Damon looked at Jeremy.

"No," Theron said. "Actually I was talking about Cyn. I'll kill her. I know where to find her. She trusts me now. She told me about this place. She told me all of you would be here tonight."

Damon's smug smile slipped away.

"You still care about Cyn," Theron told Damon. "I know you do. You could have taken her out already as your first kill, but you didn't."

Damon and the others just stared at Theron, all of them tense, all of them seemingly ready to pounce.

"I'll kill your mother, too," Theron added.

Damon's mouth twitched just a little.

"Yes," Theron said. "I know you still love your mother. You could've used her for your first kill, too. Or Jeremy's mother. Or Mel's parents. Or Ronnie's uncle. But you chose to take a runaway named Ashley Lowe as your first kill, didn't you?"

Again Damon's mouth twitched just a little.

"You didn't think I knew about Ashley Lowe? I know a lot more than you think I do."

Damon swallowed hard. He looked at Jeremy, then at Mel, then at Ronnie. They seemed to be communicating telepathically. He looked back at Theron. "I can give you the code, but you still have to be invited into the game."

"I don't care. Once I'm in, they'll see my allegiance. They'll see my loyalty, my willingness to do anything they want me to do. I just need the chance."

"Okay," Damon said. "Just relax a little, old man."

"Give me the code. Right now."

Damon waited, saying nothing.

"The code," Theron barked.

Damon looked suddenly amused. "What is it?" he asked. "Why do you want to be a vampire? What is it you're afraid of? Death? A failing heart?"

Theron's heart skipped a beat, and then began thudding in his chest. How did Damon know about his heart condition? He heard a shuffling noise behind him. He turned and saw Cyn standing there with a metal bar in her hand, already swinging it at his head, connecting.

It was too late to react. Theron felt a blast of pain and then he was out.

THIRTY-EIGHT

THERON

When Theron woke up, he found himself hanging upside down from the chain attached to the ceiling. His hands were shackled behind his back with his own handcuffs, his feet bound together with rope. The circle of blood on the floor was right underneath him. But the group of candles was no longer in the middle of the circle—now there was a large metal pan.

No, no, no, no, no . . .

Theron felt someone twist his body to the side a little, spinning him on the chain. "Wakey, wakey," a voice said—it was Jeremy.

As he twisted around on the chain, Theron felt the hands on his body again, stopping him from spinning. He saw Damon and Cyn standing in front of him. Damon had his arm draped around Cyn's shoulders. Both of them were smiling.

"When you called me from my house, I was starting to think you were on to me," Cyn told Theron. "I was afraid you were going to figure everything out, but maybe I was giving you more credit than you deserved."

"None of this is real," Theron said. "That's the truth, isn't it? You're not really vampires. None of that shit was ever real. The Vampire Game. The tasks. The rewards. You made all of that shit up. You're just killers, that's all. Isn't it?"

"I guess you'll never know," Cyn said.

"You'll get caught!" Theron screamed. "Someone will catch you eventually!" He felt his heart thudding in his chest, pulsing in his head, which felt like it was going to explode at any second from hanging upside down for so long.

"Well, it won't be you that catches us," Cyn said. She stared at him for just a moment. "It was never going to be you. You were never going to be one of us. Don't you see that?"

"Then why me? Why did you do all of this to get me here?"

"It was part of the final task," Cyn said as she pulled out a straight razor from her back pocket. "Make a non-believer a believer, and then a sacrifice." She opened the straight razor up and walked towards him. "You'll be our *next* kill, not our first."

"Ashley Lowe was your first," Theron said.

"There have been more."

"Oh God," Theron whispered. "Your family. Your mother didn't take your sisters to Ohio, did she?"

Cyn didn't answer. She was right beside Theron now with the razorblade in her hand and a wicked smile on her face.

Theron tried to thrash on the chain, but he felt the blade slice across his throat, a quick slash. There wasn't as much pain as he thought there would be. Maybe he was in shock. He felt the blood flowing immediately, felt it sliding down his face, blinding his eyes, getting into his mouth, filling his mouth with a warm coppery taste. The blood drenched his hair, dribbling down into the metal pan below, making a sound like rain drumming on a tin roof.

He had lived in a house with a tin roof when he was a child. He remembered falling asleep as he listened to the sound of rain beating on it. Theron thought of that childhood memory as the world faded away around him, as he stopped thrashing. He tried to hold on to that memory for as long as he could, and then he closed his eyes and everything went dark.

Mark Lukens

AUTHOR'S NOTE

Thank you so much for reading my book—I hope you enjoyed it!

Being an author is a dream come true for me, and it only happens because of readers like you. I thank you from the bottom of my heart.

Please feel free to follow my blog for updates, sales, articles, and more. Just enter the web address below to go to the website and then select the Follow button.

https://www.marklukensbooks.wordpress.com

ABOUT THE AUTHOR

Mark Lukens has been writing since the second grade when his teacher called his parents in for a conference because the ghost story he'd written had her a little concerned.

Since then he has had several stories published and four screenplays optioned by producers in Hollywood. He is the author of many bestselling books including: the Ancient Enemy series, Devil's Island, Sightings, The Exorcist's Apprentice, Followed, Sleep Disorders, the Dark Days series, and many more. He is a proud member of the Horror Writers Association.

He grew up in Daytona Beach, Florida. But after many travels and adventures, he settled down near Tampa, Florida with his wonderful wife and son . . . and a stray cat they adopted.

He loves to hear from readers! You can find him on Facebook here: https://www.facebook.com/Mark-Lukens-Books-670337796318510/

You can follow him on Twitter: https://www.twitter.com/marklukensbooks

His blog is: www.marklukensbooks.wordpress.com

He can be reached via email at: marklukensbooks@yahoo.com

Ancient Enemy . . . it wants things. You have to give it what it wants.

www.amazon.com/dp/B00FD4SP8M

Are aliens real? Four film school students are about to find out.

www.amazon.com/dp/B00VAI31KW

A dark collection of twelve horror stories . . . one for each month of the year.

www.amazon.com/dp/B00JENAGLC

An abandoned island with a dark and bloody past . . . an island with a terrible secret that could alter humanity forever.

www.amazon.com/dp/B06WWJC6VD

And look for the first book in my post-apocalyptic series.

www.amazon.com/dp/B07SCPL6QB

65829833R00093